Space Blasters

Also by Philip Caveney:

Night on Terror Island
Spy Another Day

SPACE BLASTERS

PHILIP CAVENEY

ANDERSEN PRESS · LONDON

First published in 2013 by
Andersen Press Limited
20 Vauxhall Bridge Road
London SW1V 2SA
www.andersenpress.co.uk

2 4 6 8 10 9 7 5 3 1

The right of Philip Caveney to be identified as the author of this work has been asserted by him in accordance with the Copyright, Designs and Patents Act, 1988.

British Library Cataloguing in Publication Data available.

ISBN 978 1 84939 572 4

Printed and bound in Great Britain by CPI Group (UK) Ltd, Croydon, CR0 4YY

For Sally Lindsay, who says she had her first kiss in the Savoy Cinema, Heaton Moor.

And for Simon Pegg, *Star Wars* fan extraordinaire.

CHAPTER ONE

Interview

It was Saturday, a day when Kip usually enjoyed what he thought of as a well-earned lie-in. But at nine o'clock sharp, Dad hammered on his bedroom door and told him to get up and dressed because somebody was coming to the house in half an hour's time, somebody he wanted Kip to meet. Kip groaned, but dragged himself blearily to the bathroom and showered himself awake.

When he finally made his way downstairs he found Dad, his dark hair combed neatly, sitting at the dining table with a skinny young woman, who was dressed in a rather hideous floral frock. She had unruly shoulder-length brown hair and wore thick, black-rimmed glasses. Having taken in her bizarre appearance, Kip noticed that she was holding a notebook and pen, and on the table in front of her was what looked like a small digital recorder. Dad's tall, gangly body was looking uncomfortable dressed in his best suit.

'Ah, Kip, perfect timing,' said Mr McCall. 'Come and meet Stephanie Holder. She's from the *Evening Post*. They're going to do a story about the *Space Blasters* launch.'

Kip tried to look positive, though he'd much rather have been tucking in to a big bowl of cornflakes right then. He pushed his dark mop of hair flat down on his head and straightened his T-shirt. He knew that his dad was excited about getting the latest *Space Blasters* film on its day of release, and he'd already told Kip that he planned to make a 'big splash' at the launch. He hadn't said anything about putting it in the newspapers though.

Kip scratched his head. 'Where're Mum and Rose?' he asked.

'They went into town, shopping for Rose's birthday present. Come and have a seat; we were just about to get started.'

Kip sat down and Stephanie grinned at him, displaying a fearsome set of multicoloured metal braces, clamped securely around both rows of her horse-like teeth.

'So you're Kip,' she said. Her voice was strange and nasal-sounding. 'Your father was just telling me all about you.'

'Was he?' Kip glanced at Dad suspiciously, wondering what he'd been saying. He took the empty seat beside him.

'Yes, he was telling me you're his right-hand man. He says that, even though you're only thirteen, sometimes you virtually run that cinema all by yourself.'

'Well, I wouldn't say that exactly.' Kip worked at the Paramount most evenings during his school holidays and had always helped out with the weekend matinees. He was proud of his involvement with the cinema, but claiming that he was running the place might be pushing it a bit.

'Makes a great story,' said Stephanie. And she wrote a few odd-looking squiggles on the pad in front of her. 'Shorthand,' she said, noticing the look of bafflement on Kip's face. 'A lost art. Hardly anyone bothers these days! So, you're still at school, I suppose?'

'Yeah, St Thomas's,' said Kip. 'Just up the road.'

'Must be handy that. Does running the cinema interfere much with your studies?'

'Well, no, not really. I only help out full time in the holidays,' explained Kip. 'During term, I just—'

'Kip's been helping me out since he was old

3

enough to walk and talk,' interrupted Dad, as though reciting a rehearsed script. 'Of course, the cinema's in his blood, you know. The Paramount has been in the McCall family since it was built by my great-grandfather in 1923.'

'Hmm,' said Stephanie, but she didn't bother writing any of that down. 'Are you an only child?' she asked Kip.

'No, I've got a sister called Rose. She's six. Seven in a couple of days.' Kip gave Stephanie a long-suffering look that seemed to say, 'Sisters, eh? What can you do with 'em?'

'Oh, so I don't suppose she'll be coming to the launch then? All that action and violence wouldn't really appeal to a seven-year-old girl.'

'She'll be there,' Dad assured her. 'The film has a 12A certificate. And she *loves* movies.'

Kip tried not to sneer. Yes, Rose liked movies all right, but only soppy ones with animated chip-munks, little ponies or dancing fairies.

Stephanie scribbled a bit more. 'I believe the Paramount is currently having a bit of a renaissance,' she said.

'Huh?' grunted Kip. His mind was still on those cornflakes.

'I think Stephanie is talking about the renovation,' explained Dad. 'Well, yes, that's true; I've invested a lot of money in the place. Mind you, we also had an anonymous donation. Back in November, somebody sent me a cheque to cover the cost of having the entire cinema steam-cleaned.'

'Really?' Stephanie looked intrigued. 'And you've honestly no idea who it was?'

'None whatsoever. There was just a note with it saying that it was to be used to pay for steam-cleaning – something I'd already been planning to do! I thought Christmas had come early!'

Kip shifted uncomfortably in his seat. He knew exactly where the money had come from . . .

'The audience figures are up too!' continued Dad. 'That's a wonderful thing in this day and age and it's why we now have the clout to get *Space Blasters* on its actual day of release. Usually, little suburban cinemas like ours have to wait weeks to get the big movies.'

'I see,' said Stephanie. 'Well done!'

'Yes, I'm very pleased about it. So I've decided to make a real effort with the launch. I've been in touch with one of those lookalike agencies. We're going to have a couple of space troopers there . . .

you know, full replica costumes, weapons, insignia, the works...'

'Cool,' said Kip.

'AND I'm arranging for an appearance by a special guest star!'

'Oh really, who's that then?' asked Stephanie.

'Can't say yet,' Dad told her, tapping the side of his nose. 'It's a *mystery* guest. All will be revealed on the big night.'

Kip looked at Dad and remembered him saying something about Sally Lovely, star of the TV soap *Corporation Road*. Sally was a local talent and Dad had recently read an interview with her, in which she said that she'd had her very first kiss in the Paramount Picture Palace. As far as Kip knew, all that Dad had done about contacting her was to send an email to the agency that represented her and he couldn't help thinking it must be more difficult than that to get her on board. Surely she'd want a fee?

Stephanie dutifully scribbled something onto her notepad. 'So,' she said, 'to what do you attribute this sudden change in the cinema's fortune?'

'Mr Lazarus,' said Kip, without thinking.

Stephanie looked at him. 'Who's Mr Lazarus?' she

asked, and Kip immediately regretted mentioning the name.

'Oh . . . he's just . . .'

'He's our projectionist,' said Dad. 'I *did* ask him to be here today, but he couldn't make it. Said he had something very important to do. I'm afraid he *can* be rather secretive.'

'Can he now?' Stephanie seemed to sit up and take notice. She wrote something on her pad and Kip had a sudden sense of misgiving.

'Yes, he's an amazing man,' said Dad, warming to his theme. 'He appeared from nowhere − just turned up out of the blue when our previous projectionist had given notice to quit. We were panicking to tell you the truth. But he took care of everything. Mr L has been in the cinema business for years, apparently, worked as an assistant to some of the great directors . . . and he has this wonderful invention called the—'

'Dad!' interrupted Kip. 'Maybe he doesn't want people to know about that.'

'Don't be daft, why wouldn't he?' Dad smiled at Stephanie. 'He calls it the Lazarus Enigma. It adds a whole new dimension to the cinema experience. Well, you'll see for yourself when you come to the launch. Naturally, I'll leave a couple of complimentary tickets at the box office for you.'

'How very kind.' Stephanie flashed her metal encrusted grin. She thought for a moment. 'So... what does it do, this... invention?'

You don't want to know, thought Kip; but he said, 'Oh, it just makes the film look a bit more... a bit more...'

'He's not exactly selling it, is he?' observed Dad. 'It's amazing, Stephanie. It makes everything look super-real. It's almost as if... well, it's almost as if you're part of the film. I think that's why people are choosing to come to us instead of the big multiplexes in town.'

'So it's like 3D?' suggested Stephanie, sounding rather unimpressed.

'It's better than 3D,' Dad assured her. 'It's an utterly immersive movie experience—'

'You were saying this Mr... What's his name again?'

'Lazarus. I think he's Italian, by birth. Used to work at a cinema in Venice, Il Fantoccini. Kip, you'll be heading to the Paramount later on, won't you? Perhaps you could arrange for Stephanie to meet up with Mr L and have a chat with him?'

'Er... I'm not sure he'd be up for that,' said Kip, worried now that it was all going a bit too far. 'He told me he had a lot of work to do before the matinee. On the Enigma.'

'Oh, I see.' Dad turned back to Stephanie. 'He spends so much time in that projection room, you'd almost swear he lives up there!'

'He doesn't, though!' said Kip, a little too loudly. 'I mean, that would be mental, wouldn't it? Living in a projection room! As if!'

Stephanie gave him an odd look, but Dad just carried on, oblivious. 'I really think it would be worth you talking to him. The stories that man can tell about the film business, well, they'd fill a book.'

Stephanie smiled. 'Do you have contact details for him?' she asked. 'Perhaps I'll look him up before I start writing.'

'Well, you can generally get him on the phone at the cinema. You already have that number. He doesn't have a mobile. Can you believe that? No mobile in this day and age! And his address... let me think now...' Dad dutifully reeled off the false address that Mr Lazarus had given him back when he first started work, and Kip's sense of dread deepened. What if Stephanie called by to see him? She'd realise the place didn't even exist.

'You know what, I don't think it's worth bothering,' said Kip. 'Honestly. He's really not that interesting.'

Dad stared at him. 'What are you on about?' he cried. 'You're always telling me some amazing story you've got from him.'

'Yeah, but ... but ... it's like you said, Dad, he's secretive and ... and he won't want to answer a load of questions.'

'Oh, don't you worry,' said Stephanie. 'Secrets are my speciality. If he's got some, I'm just the one to worm them out of him.' She smiled knowingly. 'We journalists always get our story in the end.'

Kip tried not to groan. In trying to play things down, he'd probably made it worse.

'Anyway,' said Stephanie. 'When does this shin-dig kick off?'

'Friday night at eight p.m.,' said Dad.

'Perfect. Our next issue is out on Thursday. I think I can promise you a full page ... maybe even a two-page spread if Mr Lazarus is as interesting as you say he is. Anything else I need to know?'

Kip wondered what she'd say if he spilled the beans.

'*Actually, yes, there is. Mr Lazarus is over one hundred and twenty years old. He has a business card that plays film images. He could send you – flowery dress, teeth braces and all – into a film about Roman gladiators so you could be chopped to pieces in an arena; he probably will do if you start asking too many questions . . .*'

But, of course, Kip couldn't say any of that. He just smiled, shook his head and sat in his chair as Stephanie said her goodbyes and packed away her little recorder. Dad showed her to the door and then came back, rubbing his hands, a big smile on his face.

'Well,' he said. 'I think that went rather well, don't you?'

CHAPTER TWO

An Argument

As soon as he'd wolfed down some breakfast, Kip made an excuse, let himself out of the house and hurried into the village to the Paramount Picture Palace. He wanted to warn Mr Lazarus of the potential trouble from this journalist. It was the last thing they needed, just when everything was going so well.

He paused for a moment to gaze at the cinema, marvelling at the changes that had occurred in just one short year. Previously a scruffy little fleapit with missing tiles and leaking gutters, the Paramount now gleamed from top to bottom. Funded by a dramatic rise in audience numbers, it had been fully refurbished inside and out. Tiles had been replaced, gutters repaired, seats and carpets steam-cleaned until they looked as good as new. The Paramount's changing fortunes had meant that things had improved at home too. The Christmas presents had been pretty spectacular this year, and Mum and Dad hadn't been too sniffy when Rose had pleaded with them to buy her a mobile phone for her birthday. Kip couldn't help feeling annoyed. He'd had to wait until he was twelve before he'd been allowed a pay-as-you-go phone.

It was all thanks to Mr Lazarus, of course. When the mysterious projectionist had come to work at the cinema, he'd brought with him his brilliant invention, the Lazarus Enigma, a device that did more than just enhance films as Dad had told Stephanie. It could put you into them – really transport you into the film's story, so you could interact with the characters. You could even take out memorabilia from the film. That was how Kip had paid for the steam-clean of the cinema. He'd taken Jason Corder's ID card from the film *Spy Another Day* and Mr Lazarus had sold it to a collector. But you had to be careful because when you were in a film, everything was real – real people, real weapons, real peril – and if you didn't get out before the final credits rolled, you'd be trapped in there for ever, doomed to do the same crazy things over and over again, for the rest of your days.

Kip knew this better than anyone. So far he'd gone into three movies and in each case he'd been lucky to get out alive. You'd have thought that would be enough to put anybody off, and yet . . .

Dominating the display boards at the front of the cinema was a massive full-colour poster for the latest *Space Blasters* film – *The Emperor's Revenge*. The poster depicted the film's youthful hero, Zeke Stardancer, standing in an action pose, his powerful plasma gun raised, while one brawny arm encircled the waist of his regular love interest, Princess Shanna. Kip gazed up at the poster with mixed feelings. The *Space Blasters* series was one of his all-time favourites, and part of him would love to go into outer space and share a mission with his intergalactic heroes . . . but after the nightmare adventure he'd suffered in the monster movie, *Terror Island*, and the deadly games he'd been forced to endure in *Spy Another Day*, he'd told himself that nothing – absolutely nothing – would ever entice him to go into a movie again.

His girlfriend Beth felt the same way about it. It almost shocked him to think of her as 'his girlfriend' but he supposed that was what she was now. She'd been the one who'd persuaded him to go into the spy movie – mostly so she could meet her heart-throb, Daniel Crag – but the mission had not gone smoothly, and even she'd had to admit that Crag's screen persona, the ice-cool super spy, Jason Corder, wasn't anything like as nice as she'd expected.

Still, it cost nothing to fantasise and for a moment Kip allowed himself to imagine sitting at the controls of the *Trillenium Hawk*, Stardancer's legendary spacecraft, guiding it through an asteroid field while he took out enemy spaceships with lethal blasts from his laser cannon.

Kip sighed and forced himself to push the thought away. From now on, no matter what enticements Mr Lazarus offered him, he was staying out of the movies for good and contenting himself with simply watching them.

He climbed the steps to the entrance and reached for his keys to unlock the swing door, but hesitated. The catch had not been secured, which was unusual. As Dad had jokingly touched on, Mr Lazarus did live up in the projection room where he kept his precious film props and memorabilia, and he was usually very careful to ensure that the entrance was always kept locked. Kip pushed open the door and stepped into the lobby. He turned the lock behind him and made his way across the foyer, but paused when he heard the sound of distant voices shouting. Was the Paramount being burgled or something? He concentrated for a moment and thought that he recognised one of the voices as that of Mr Lazarus.

He pushed through the swing doors at the far end of the room into the auditorium. He climbed the flight of steps beyond and turned to look up at the steeply angled seats at the rear of the cinema. The voices were louder now but still muffled and he realised they were coming from the projection room. He moved quickly and quietly up the steps until he was standing just a few metres away from the half-open door. Peering through, he could see Mr Lazarus's back, clad in his usual outfit of a white shirt, black leather waistcoat and pinstripe trousers. He appeared to be in the middle of a row with a stranger – a fat man with dyed curly black hair and a straggly bootlace moustache. He was dressed in a grey leather jacket, jeans and what looked like a pair of cowboy boots. Despite the intruder's massive size, he shared some features with the far skinnier Mr Lazarus. He had the same cold grey eyes, though his were set deep in a red, chubby face, and there was something similar about the thin-lipped mouth. Like Mr Lazarus, the stranger looked maybe fifty or sixty years old, but something about him gave the impression that he was almost certainly much older. He also had an Italian accent, but his was gruffer and less lilting than the man he was arguing with.

'I can't believe it,' he snarled. 'I ask you to do this one thing for me, and you tell me it's out of the question. Why? What skin is it off your nose?'

'That's not the point,' replied Mr Lazarus. 'I have helped you many times and I will do so again, whenever you need it, you know that. I think the elixir should be enough, but it never is, is it, Dario? Always there is something else you want from me and always it is the one thing I cannot give you.' Mr Lazarus sounded angry.

'Hasn't anybody ever told you that blood is thicker than water?' countered the stranger. 'You owe me this favour.'

'I owe you nothing!' Mr Lazarus shook a gloved fist at the man. 'When you turned up in Scotland, I went against all my better judgement and gave you what you asked for. You promised me you would never ask again – but here we are, just twelve months down the line, and the song hasn't changed.' Mr Lazarus adopted a pitiful wheedling tone. 'Help me, Matteus, help me! I'm in big trouble!'

Kip frowned. *Matteus!* In the year that Kip had known Mr Lazarus, the old man had never revealed his first name. How odd to hear it after all this time.

The fat man scowled. 'I don't understand what the big deal is,' he said. 'It wouldn't cost you one penny and you'd be rid of me for good.'

'I seem to remember you said that the last time! But it's wrong to take more than you need. You notice I'm not exactly living in luxury here.' He waved a gloved hand at the crowded interior of the projection room – the ancient equipment, the stuffed animals, the ever-bubbling coffee machine. 'You think I've never been tempted? Of course I have. But I resist!'

Kip had to admit this was true. The only things Mr L ever asked Kip to bring out of the films were little trinkets. Oh, they were worth serious money to movie-mad collectors, but nothing compared to the riches he could bring back to the real world if he so desired.

'Then do this thing I ask of you and share the rewards with me. We'd be set up for life, Matteus. We'd be rich beyond our wildest dreams!'

'No, Dario, it's not how I operate, it never has been. You don't understand, do you? I only take what I need to survive and, for me, that's enough. Why can't you understand that?'

Kip decided he'd heard enough. He cleared his throat, rather louder than was strictly necessary, and the man called Dario lifted his gaze to stare at Kip through the open doorway, his aloof expression suggesting he didn't much care for what he saw. Mr Lazarus spun round and stared at Kip in evident dismay.

'Kip!' he gasped. 'What are you doing here?'

Kip took a hesitant step forward. 'I . . . just called round to see you. I heard voices. Do you know you left the front door unlocked?'

'Did I?' Mr Lazarus looked perturbed. 'I'm sorry, I was a little . . . flustered.' It was strange to see Mr Lazarus like this. He was usually so calm and assured.

Dario grinned. 'Who's this pipsqueak?' he asked, waving a hand in Kip's direction. 'Your new employer?' He laughed unpleasantly. 'He looks a little young to be giving the orders.'

'My employer's *son*,' Mr Lazarus corrected him. 'A good friend of mine.' He stared at Dario. 'I won't detain you any longer,' he said. 'I'm sure you must be very busy.' He glanced back at Kip. 'My brother was just leaving.'

'Your...brother?' Kip stared at Mr Lazarus in amazement. 'I didn't know you had a—'

'Oh, so he's not mentioned me, then?' said Dario. He shook his head and tutted loudly. 'Matteus, I'm offended. I would have thought you'd be proud to tell everyone about your little brother. After everything we've been through together, surely you owe me that much?'

There was a long silence while the two men stared at each other.

'I'll show you out,' said Mr Lazarus at last, taking a bunch of keys from his waistcoat pocket; it was plain that as far as he was concerned, this was the end of the conversation. Dario shrugged his shoulders but he obeyed the command, pushing his big body roughly past Kip's slight one and almost knocking him over in the process.

Mr Lazarus gave Kip an apologetic look as he went past. 'Wait for me,' he murmured. 'I'll explain.' He followed Dario down the steps to the exit and the two men disappeared out into the foyer.

Kip was left in the empty projection room, feeling rather awkward and wondering why Mr Lazarus had kept his brother a secret for a whole year.

He didn't have to wait long to find out.

CHAPTER THREE

Dario

Five minutes later, Mr Lazarus was back. He ushered Kip to a seat at the small table and busied himself at his beloved Gaggia coffee machine, making Kip a latte.

'I can't stay long,' Kip warned him. 'I've got stuff to do before the matinee this afternoon.'

Mr Lazarus either ignored or didn't hear what Kip had said. 'I'm sorry you had to witness that,' he said as he steam-heated milk in a tall glass.

'That's OK,' Kip assured him. 'It's just funny that you never mentioned him before . . . What's his name? Dario?'

Mr Lazarus kept his back turned, but from the tone of his voice Kip could tell that he was frowning. 'I didn't mention him because Dario is trouble. Always has been.'

'He said he was your *little* brother?'

'Yes. He is five years younger than me.'

Kip wasn't really sure what that meant. He knew

21

that Mr Lazarus was really over one hundred and twenty years old, so ... Mr Lazarus seemed to understand his confusion.

'Obviously I have helped him over the years. You remember I told you about the film I go into from time to time? The one that keeps me looking younger? Like me, Dario is a traveller. He visits places all over the world, usually because he's on the run from somebody he owes money to. From time to time, he looks me up and I send him into the film so he can wipe away the years. You should have seen what he looked like when he arrived here an hour ago! He looked every one of his ...' He thought for a moment as though counting in his head. '... one hundred and seventeen years.'

The projectionist turned away from the machine and brought two coffees over to the table. He looked worried, Kip thought. Worried and tired.

'Is that the special film?' asked Kip. He pointed to a strip of old celluloid which was still threaded through the projector.

Mr Lazarus nodded. 'It's very precious,' he said. 'Like myself, it's more than a hundred years old. I'm sure you know that old film stock is highly flammable. I have to be so careful with it.'

Kip sipped at his latte, which as ever, was absolutely delicious. 'So . . . if you do all that for your brother, why the argument?'

Mr Lazarus sighed. 'Because, as always, he wanted more. You have to understand, Dario and I have never got along. As a child, he was always getting into trouble, causing fights, quarrelling with the local gangs, setting fire to things . . . If there was any kind of trouble you could guarantee that he would be involved! As he got older, we seemed to drift further and further apart. I found my vocation in the world of the cinema and he . . .' Mr Lazarus shook his head. 'He found his in the world of crime.'

Kip nearly choked on his latte. 'He's a gangster?' he cried.

Mr Lazarus forced a thin smile. 'Perhaps that is too strong a word,' he said. 'Dario has always been drawn to the darker side of society. What he likes best of all is gambling.'

'What, you mean, like making bets and stuff?'

Mr Lazarus nodded. 'With Dario, it's mostly card games. He's what is known as a compulsive gambler. He just cannot help himself. Wherever he goes, he falls in with the wrong crowd, he plays cards for money and, of course, in the end he loses. Then he has to leave wherever it is he's living and start all over again. Usually he begins by tracking me down. He goes into the film and wipes away all the wrinkles and illnesses he's acquired since I last saw him...'

'How does that work exactly?' Kip had always wondered, and today Mr L seemed to be in a sharing mood.

Mr Lazarus thought for a moment. 'Let me see now... I think it was in the early 1900s... I took a year off from my duties with George Melies and travelled to England to work as an assistant to a young director called James Williamson. We worked on several projects together and one of them was a film called *The Elixir of Youth*. Just a short silent movie, maybe three minutes long. There is only one copy of that film in existence and I have it. The film....' He broke off as a thought seemed to occur to him. He stood up, walked to the projector and carefully rewound the film to the beginning. 'An image is worth a thousand words,' he said.

A flickering black and white image appeared on the screen: a bearded man standing beside a table, which was set up in front of a mirror. The man was dressed as a magician with a turban and a long beaded cloak. On the table stood a small bottle.

'The bottle is supposed to contain something called Amrita,' explained Mr Lazarus, 'the name that the Indians gave to the Elixir of Youth. Have you ever heard of it before?'

Kip shook his head, concentrating on the action in front of him. Now an actor stepped onto the stage, walking with the aid of a stick, a stooped wizened old fellow with grey hair and a long beard. He handed the magician a coin and the man made a flamboyant bow and pointed to the bottle. The actor picked up the bottle and drank from it. He stood for a moment as if feeling some kind of an effect. Then there was a puff of smoke and suddenly he had changed to a young, clean-shaven fellow, with a straight back. He threw aside his stick and went dancing merrily off screen. The magician bowed, the screen flickered and went blank.

A simple enough trick, Kip decided. The actor was obviously a young man made up to look old. At a certain point the director would simply have stopped the camera. The actor would have removed his make-up, his false beard and grey wig, then resumed his position while the cameraman started filming again, letting off a smoke bomb at the same moment. He knew it was how most special effects were achieved in the silent movie era.

'Primitive stuff, but very effective,' said Mr Lazarus. 'Unfortunately, Williamson wasn't pleased with the way the film was processed. Did you notice anything odd about it?'

Kip thought for a moment – the lighting had been odd. 'It was a little over-exposed,' he said.

'Excellent!' said Mr Lazarus. 'You have a good eye, Kip. Yes, Williamson noticed that too and he was particular about such things. He gave me the roll of film for safekeeping. Then he shot another version of the idea and called it *The Elixir Of Life* and *that* was the one that was released. I went back to Italy and took his film with me. It wasn't till years later, long after Williamson was dead, that I remembered it . . . I'd kept it safe over the passing years, thinking that perhaps one day somebody would want to see it again.

'Then many, many years later, when I had invented the Lazarus Enigma, it occurred to me that a man could easily go into that film and drink from the bottle. All I had to do was get there just before the original actor! Even though the bottle contained nothing more than tap water, I realised that the

Enigma would make it real, would turn it into actual Amrita. The first time I tried it I was in my late seventies. I went into the film and I saw my reflection in the mirror. There was an old man, greying and stooped. I drank from the bottle and the reflection changed. Instantly I was young again, all my infirmities gone.' He was wide-eyed as he spoke, recalling the wonder of it all. 'Each time I go in, the bottle is full again. I drink, the years drop away and I am the man you see before you.'

'Couldn't you bring the bottle out of the film?' asked Kip. 'Then you'd have it handy, whenever you needed it.'

Mr Lazarus shook his head. 'It's only a small bottle. It would work well enough if I brought it out, but it wouldn't replenish itself in the real world. No, it has to be kept in the film and the film has to be protected at all costs. If anything ever happened to it . . .' He shook his head as though he couldn't bring himself to mention the consequences, but Kip got the general idea. If something happened to the film, Mr Lazarus would soon start to look his real age. The effects would be fatal.

'And Dario?' he asked. 'How does he come into this?'

Mr Lazarus sighed. 'One day, when I was working at the cinema in Venice, he came to visit me. Just turned up out of the blue. He was frail and ill. It was a shock to see how much he'd aged. He was amazed to see how young and fit I looked and begged to know my secret. I took pity on him and allowed him to go into my film and drink from the bottle. I told him that any time he wanted to return for another taste, all he had to do was contact me. I gave him the gift of immortality and I thought that should have been enough but, just as soon as he came out of the film, he asked me for the favour.'

'The favour?'

Mr Lazarus picked up his cup of strong, black coffee in his gloved hands and took a sip, grimacing as the bitter liquid went down.

'Oh, it was just some crackpot get-rich scheme. It always is. You see, he understood very quickly how the Enigma works, how it can make the most incredible things real. He had run up some debts at the gaming tables and wanted me to make him rich by allowing him to go into another film and plunder. Over the years he hasn't changed. His latest scheme? He wants to go into one of those pirate movies.' He laughed dismissively. 'In the new one, he tells me, the heroes find this fabulous treasure, a whole room packed full of it: diamonds, rubies, gold and silver! His plan is to grab as much of it as he can carry and bring it back. And then it will be...'

'*Real* treasure,' murmured Kip. 'Wow!'

'But, of course, I told him I wouldn't do it.'

'No?' Kip tried not to sound disappointed.

'Of course not! You have seen how I operate, Kip. Yes, occasionally I bring back little items for my collector friends. Jason Corder's ID card...'

'John Dillinger's hat!' Kip reminded him of the collector's item he had been persuaded to go into *Public Enemy Number One* for.

'Yes, yes, trinkets. Items that become real, and which I can sell to help me to continue my valuable work. Don't forget, this cinema itself has benefitted from some of those sales. That steam-cleaning didn't come cheap! But to set myself up as a rich man?' He shook his head. 'That would be against all my principles. Also...if I were to allow Dario to do this thing, what do you suppose would be the result?'

Kip shrugged. 'He'd get rich?' he suggested.

'Not for long. The more money that Dario has, the more he is drawn to gamble it away and the more trouble he ends up in. It's a vicious circle. So you see, I'm really doing him a favour by saying no.'

Kip frowned. 'I don't expect he sees it that way,' he said.

Mr Lazarus sighed. 'All the same, this is how it has to be. The problem is, once Dario gets an idea into his head, it's hard to talk him out of it. He'll keep on and on at me in the hope that I'll somehow change my mind.' He stared bleakly across the room at the rickety-looking piece of machinery that stood beside the film projector. Kip followed his gaze. The Lazarus Enigma wasn't very much to look at: a roughly made wooden platform on wheels, mounted on a short stretch of metal track. But Kip knew, when a person stood on the platform and it was pushed forward until the light reflected through the prism mounted above it, they would experience a sudden melting sensation – and then they would be in the film, interacting with the characters, who were no longer actors but the real thing.

Looking at the Enigma seemed to remind Mr Lazarus of something. He studied Kip for a moment. 'I was thinking,' he said. 'You're a big *Space Blasters* fan, aren't you?'

'Er...yeah...' agreed Kip, cautiously. This was an understatement. Back at home, Kip had a huge collection of books and posters relating to the series, and all the DVDs.

'One of my collectors has asked me if it would be possible to get hold of one of the laser swords they use in those films.'

'Oh yes?' Kip could see exactly where this was going.

'I was just wondering if by any chance—'

'No,' interrupted Kip. 'No, Mr Lazarus. I'm sorry, but there's no chance at all, not after last time.'

Mr Lazarus looked offended. 'You haven't even heard me out!' he protested.

'I know exactly what you're going to say,' Kip told him. He adopted a shonky Italian accent. 'Oh, Keep, Keep, just do this one thing for me! Don't worry, I will send you into a safe part of the feelm, you'll be een and out in five minutes!'

Mr Lazarus looked offended. 'There's no need to be rude,' he said. 'I was only asking.'

'And I'm just telling you. Never again! It's funny how you never seem to want to go into the films yourself.'

'I've told you a hundred times. Film characters

31

are so much less wary of children turning up out of the blue. An old fellow like myself would never get their trust the way that you do.' He thought for a moment. 'Perhaps if I were to ask Beth . . .'

'NO! She feels the same way about it. We were nearly killed last time. So were you, for that matter. Surely you must have learned your lesson by now?'

'We could learn from the mistakes we made last time.'

'You always say that – then you go and make a load of new ones!'

'Kip, if you'll just listen for . . .'

'No, Mr Lazarus. I'm sorry, but that's it.' Kip thought for a moment. 'It's not as if we need the money now, is it? The Paramount is doing really well and I know for a fact that Dad gave you a pay rise to say thank you for all the help you've given him.'

Mr Lazarus glared at him. 'How do you know about that?' he demanded.

'I overheard him telling you. I have got ears, you know! So, the only reason you could have for sending me and Beth back into a movie is because . . . because you somehow enjoy doing it. And I'm sorry, but that's not enough of a reason.' Kip glanced at his watch and took a last gulp of his latte. 'I need to get back,' he said. 'I've got homework to do before the matinee this afternoon.' A thought occurred to him. He'd been so caught up in Mr Lazarus's story he'd forgotten his reason for coming here in the first place. 'Listen, I came here to warn you. Dad had this woman round the house this morning, a reporter for the local paper. She started asking questions.'

Mr Lazarus looked nervous. 'Questions?' he muttered. 'What kind of questions?'

'About you. And about the Enigma. She wants to talk to you.'

'Well, I hope you told her I'm a busy man.'

'Yeah, of course I did. Didn't seem to put her off though. Her name's Stephanie Holder. So, if she gets in touch with you . . .'

'Oh, don't worry,' said Mr Lazarus, with a dismissive wave of his hand. 'I know these journalists. Most of them are really quite dim. I'll handle her.'

'Hmm.' Kip was unconvinced. 'Well, all I'm saying is, watch out. And don't go shooting your mouth off without thinking it through first. Everything's great here now and we don't want to spoil it, do we? Now I really should get back.'

'And you'll let me know about *Space Blasters*?'

'I've already told you,' Kip assured him. 'I'm not doing it.'

Mr Lazarus looked glum. 'Well,' he said, 'if that's how you feel about it.' Then he turned and gave Kip a cunning look. 'But think about it for just a moment,' he added, his eyes flashing with mischief. '*Space Blasters*. Rocket ships, laser swords, aliens and robots. Wouldn't it be . . . what's the word you youngsters use these days? Cool! Wouldn't it be really cool?'

And for a moment, Kip couldn't help but picture himself back at the controls of the *Trillenium Hawk*, hurtling through outer space in a desperate struggle for survival against his alien adversaries. He made an effort to pull himself together. 'I'll see you later,' he said and headed for the door.

'At least think about it!' shouted Mr Lazarus, but by that time Kip was out of the door and heading down the stairs, as fast as his legs could carry him.

Chapter Four

The Noose Tightens

Kip walked out onto the brilliantly lit stage. He was surprised to find himself here. In front of him a man stood beside a small table, which had been placed before a mirror. The man wore an orange turban and a full-length gown, which glittered with sequins and jewels. Kip had expected it to be the same actor he'd seen before, but when he looked, the man had a chubby red face and a straggly bootleg moustache, and Kip realised that it was Dario, Mr Lazarus's brother. He bowed theatrically and gestured to the table, where a small bottle stood. Kip gazed at the bottle. It had a white label and written on it, in fancy old-fashioned letters, was the word AMRITA. Kip knew what he was supposed to do. He reached out, picked up the bottle and lifted it to his lips. Then he took a long swig from the contents.

Oddly, it tasted like Dandelion & Burdock. Kip could feel it coursing its way down his gullet and into his belly. He set the bottle down on the table and then studied his reflection in the mirror behind it. His face gazed back at him with an apprehensive expression. Now he could feel something rumbling in his stomach, a strange blossoming warmth that seemed to be spreading outwards, glowing in his chest, seeping into his arms and legs.

And then, in the mirror, he saw that his face was beginning to change. But something was wrong. His eyes seemed to sink deeper into his skull, the smooth white skin on his forehead furrowed and creased, the lines on either side of his nose seemed to etch themselves deeper, his pink lips turned pale and the skin began to crack and wither. Most shocking of all, his thick black hair began to turn pale and grey and then faded from the top of his head completely, revealing his bare scalp.

Horrified, he turned to look at Dario, only to find that he had been replaced by Mr Lazarus, who was laughing at Kip's plight.

'Help me,' croaked Kip. He lifted a hand to beg and saw that it had turned into a withered, liver-spotted claw.

Kip woke with a gasp of terror and lay there for a moment, trying to get his breath back. The dream had seemed so real. He stared up at the ceiling and then got another shock as a head moved into view. He realised that somebody was standing beside his bed in the half-light, gazing down at him. He snapped out a hand and switched on his bedside lamp, to reveal Dad – wearing his pyjamas, his hair ruffled from sleep. He didn't look very happy.

'What... what's wrong?' croaked Kip. He glanced at his *Space Blasters* alarm clock. 'Dad, it's only seven o'clock. I always have a lie-in on Sundays.'

Dad nodded, but he lifted a brown envelope and showed it to Kip.

'Recognise this?' he asked.

Kip stared at it, a sinking feeling in his stomach. 'It... looks like an... envelope,' he said slowly.

'Yes. The one Mr Lazarus gave me when he started work here.'

'Dad, that was a year ago!'

'I know. But try to remember. I asked him for references?'

A dull wave of memory pulsed through Kip. Yes, he knew about that envelope. He had gone through it when Mr Lazarus first started at the Paramount. Dad hadn't got around to looking at it but Kip had and knew only too well what was in there. He was also surprised that Dad had managed to find it. Kip had taken great care to bury it at the bottom of a heap of paperwork in Dad's study.

'Oh, yeah, I remember that,' said Kip, trying to sound casual, even though his heart was beating like a mallet in his chest. 'It was all in Italian. I didn't think you'd be interested.'

Dad frowned and sat on the edge of the bed.

'I only remembered him giving it to me late last night,' he said. 'I thought there might be something useful in there for Stephanie's article. Something she might be able to use. I couldn't get back to sleep this morning so I got up and went to find it. It took me ages; it was buried under a pile of other stuff.' He gave Kip a suspicious look and Kip made an effort not to look guilty – not easy when he was half asleep.

'Dad, I really could do with a bit more shuteye. Could we maybe talk about this later?'

Dad ignored him. He reached into the envelope and withdrew a picture, which he handed to Kip. 'What d'you make of that?' he asked.

Kip wasn't surprised; he'd known exactly which picture it would be. The one that had first given him pause for thought about Mr Lazarus. It was an old black and white photograph showing a bunch of people on the steps of a cinema. Above the door, the name of the cinema was etched into the stone. Il Fantoccini. And below that, on the hording, was the name of the film that was being premiered there. *Cabiria*. And standing to one side of the moustachioed man who was evidently the owner, stood a handsome young fellow in a white shirt, leather waistcoat and striped trousers. Dad pointed a finger.

'Tell me that's not Mr Lazarus,' he said.

Kip stared at the photograph in silence for a moment, trying to gather his thoughts. 'It . . . looks a bit like him,' he admitted. 'But . . .'

'A bit?' roared Dad. 'That's his double. He even dresses the same, right down to the gloves.'

'Dad, shhh!' hissed Kip. 'You'll wake Mum and Rose.'

'Never mind that. See the film title there . . . *Cabiria*. A film that was released in 1914. I know, I checked. And that looks like its premiere.'

'Yeah, but that doesn't mean . . .'

'The guy in the picture is maybe twenty years old, right? Which by my reckoning makes Mr Lazarus over a hundred and twenty,' concluded Dad. 'And he looks maybe fifty or sixty, tops.'

'Dad, that's mental,' said Kip. 'He couldn't be that old. Nobody could.'

'That's what I've been telling myself,' said Dad, 'over and over. There must be some mistake, there has to be. But that interview yesterday, it got me thinking. Why *is* he so secretive? Why does he never seem to leave the cinema? And why were you so anxious to play him down when we were speaking to Stephanie? Almost as though you *know* something.'

Just then, the bedroom door opened and Rose wandered in, a look of annoyance on her face. Wearing her pink princess pyjamas, her golden hair plaited, she was clutching her favourite teddy bear, Malcolm, and rubbing her eyes.

'What's going on?' she cried, resentfully. 'You woke me up!'

'Go back to bed,' Kip advised her. The last thing he needed right now was Rose poking her nose into things. She was already suspicious enough about Mr Lazarus.

'Will not. What are you two shouting about?'

'We're just talking about Mr Lazarus,' said Dad, calmly.

Rose made a face. 'Him,' she said. 'He's a *weirdo*.'

40

Dad looked at her with interest. 'What makes you say that?' he asked her.

She came over to the bed and sat beside Dad, slipping an arm around his waist. 'He's always doing funny stuff up in that film room place,' she said.

'The projection room?' Dad scowled. 'What kind of funny stuff?'

'I don't know exactly,' said Rose. 'But Kip and Beth spend all their time with him in there and once they came out all muddy and their clothes were torn and Kip's best shoes were burned on the bottom.'

Kip felt himself beginning to panic. The secrets that he'd kept for the best part of a year were in danger of being revealed.

Dad stared at Rose for a moment, and then directed his gaze at Kip. 'Well?' he said.

'I don't know what she's on about,' protested Kip. 'Burned shoes! I think somebody's been having bad dreams again.'

'They *were* burned! Daddy didn't notice, but I did. You threw them in the bin before Mum could see them!'

'I . . . trod in some dog muck,' Kip said quickly. 'It wouldn't wash off.'

'Never mind about the shoes,' growled Dad. 'What about Mr Lazarus?'

'Well, I ... sometimes me and Beth go and help him work on the Enigma, that's all. Oiling it, making little changes. And ... and he tells us stories and stuff about the old days ... He's cool, Mr L, he's ... he's our mate. And, OK maybe he does seem a bit weird sometimes, but that's just cos he ... he's spent his entire life making movies and stuff, he doesn't get out much.'

'Have you ever been to his flat?' asked Dad.

'No, never.'

Dad frowned. 'It's weird. I remember now, I was going to send his pay to the address he gave me and when I tried to arrange it, he said he'd prefer to be paid in cash. Whenever I say I'll send him something he always has some excuse. "Bring it to the Paramount," that's what he always says. I've been thinking since the interview. All that junk he keeps up in the projection room. Crammed with stuff, it is. There's even a folding bed. It's almost as though ... as though ...'

'What?' asked Kip.

Dad laughed. 'I know it sounds ridiculous but ... he couldn't ... I mean, Kip, he couldn't actually be *living* up there, could he?'

Kip forced a laugh and hoped it sounded more convincing than it felt. 'You're joking, right? You think he lives in the projection room?'

'I know it sounds crazy but...'

'And this?' He pointed at the picture. 'You think this is *him*? This is his granddad! Yeah, he told me once, that's how he got the job at Il Fanto...Il Fanto...this place! His granddad worked there for years before him, and his father too. It was like the Paramount, you know, a family business.' Kip went for an angle he knew his dad liked. 'When Mr L was a teenager, his dad trained him up to take over the job, just like you're training me. They all dressed the same way. It was a kind of gimmick.'

Dad seemed to visibly relax at Kip's lies, as though somebody had pulled a cord in his back. Rose however, did not look quite so convinced. She glared at the photograph. 'He's got the same eyes,' she said. 'The same nose, the same teeth, the same...'

'Yes, all right, Rose, we get the general idea,' said Dad. 'Of course that has to be it. His grandfather. Now you've said it, it's obvious. I'm being paranoid. People used to tell me all the time how much like

my dad I looked. As if anybody could be that old!'
He laughed and shook his head. Then he took the
photograph and slid it back into the envelope. 'Sorry
to have disturbed you,' he said. 'I must be going
loopy in my old age.' He stood up and beckoned to
Rose. 'Come on,' he said. 'Let's get you back to bed.
Maybe you can grab another hour or two.'

He started for the door and Rose followed, but
she hesitated for a moment and looked back at Kip,
her expression cool. 'You've got Daddy fooled,' she
said quietly. 'But not me.'

Then she went out, closing the door behind her.

Kip let out a long sigh and lay down again. He
was off the hook for the moment, but he knew
Rose, and once she got her teeth into something
she never let go. He closed his eyes but, not
surprisingly, he didn't get any more sleep.

CHAPTER FIVE

The Deal

After a quick breakfast that seemed to lie in his stomach like a pile of rocks, Kip went back to his room and phoned Beth's mobile. It rang for quite a while before she answered.

'H'lo?' She sounded sleepy, and Kip realised he'd woken her up.

'It's me,' he hissed, not wanting to be overheard by anyone. 'Look, something's happened. Can you meet me at the top of the road in ten?'

'What's the matter?' she asked him.

'I'll explain on the way to the Paramount.'

'It's a bit early for that, isn't it?' Beth usually came along to help with the Sunday matinee at two o' clock, but it wasn't yet eight thirty. 'Make it twenty minutes,' she grumbled. 'I need to eat something.'

'OK, just be there,' he said and hung up. Twenty minutes later, he got to the top of the road and found Beth waiting for him, looking more than a bit put out. She was dressed in jeans and a T-shirt and her normally immaculate hair was messy and unwashed. 'This had better be important,' she told him irritably. 'I barely had time to eat my toast.'

'Never mind about that,' said Kip. He held his thumb and forefinger slightly apart. 'This morning, Dad came *this close* to finding out the truth about Mr Lazarus.'

'Oh,' said Beth. She frowned. 'I suppose it was bound to come out sooner or later. I mean, your dad's not exactly Sherlock Holmes, but this has been going on under his nose for what . . . a year?' They started walking down to the cinema and Kip filled Beth in on everything that had happened the day before, from meeting Dario to being woken up by Dad again this morning and all points in between. 'So, what's this Darius like?' she asked him when he'd finished talking.

'Dario,' Kip corrected her. 'I only saw him for a moment, but Mr L says he's trouble.'

'Well, he ought to know,' said Beth. 'Being the expert on trouble.'

They got to the Paramount and Kip unlocked the door. They went in, locking up after themselves, and made their way to the projection room. Kip tapped on the door and a small voice inside said, 'Come.'

They found Mr Lazarus sitting at his table, contemplating a half drunk cup of coffee. He looked up at them and smiled, but it was tight lipped and unconvincing. He was clearly worried. 'You two are early,' he observed and his voice was as flat and dull as his expression. 'Let me get you both a drink.'

'I'll see to that,' said Beth. She nodded to Kip. 'You give him the news.'

Kip sighed. He sat down opposite Mr Lazarus.

'Good news, I hope,' said Mr Lazarus.

Kip shook his head and told him what had happened that morning.

'Oh dear,' said Mr Lazarus when Kip had finished talking. 'Oh dear, oh dear.'

'Is that all you've got to say?' cried Kip.

'What else *can* I say?'

'You could maybe think about what we're going to do to sort it out,' said Kip. 'I talked Dad round to believing that it's your granddad in that picture... but Rose didn't go for it, not for one minute, and she can twist Dad round her little finger when she puts her mind to it. And then there's that Stephanie to think about.'

'Stephanie Holder,' said Mr Lazarus glumly. 'From the *Evening Post*.'

'She's been in touch?'

'She phoned me yesterday.'

'Oh, great. What did she want?'

'To ask me questions,' said Mr Lazarus. 'Lots of questions. About me, my life, my history. When was I born, where was I born . . . ?'

'You didn't tell her, did you?' asked Kip anxiously.

'Of course not. I'm not that stupid! No, I made something up. But I'm not good with numbers and I started contradicting myself.'

'That isn't like you,' said Beth. 'You're usually so calm and in control of things.'

'I know,' agreed Mr Lazarus woefully. 'But since Dario appeared on the scene, I seem to have gone to pieces. My brother always has this effect on me.'

'So what did you say to Stephanie?' asked Kip.

'I don't know what I said. She asked me so many questions I was dizzy with them! Then she said she wanted to send down a photographer but I said I was going out for the evening.' He frowned. 'It was all most unpleasant. She sounded like a real snoop.'

'I suppose that's her job,' said Beth.

'She's going to find out,' said Kip. 'She's going to check out that address and realise it's not even a real place.'

48

'But . . . it's not as if I'm doing anything wrong,' pleaded Mr Lazarus.

'Yes you are,' said Beth, bringing the drinks to the table. 'You're living in a projection room, for a start. There's bound to be some kind of law that says you can't do that. I mean, look at this place. It doesn't even have a window! And it's not like you're paying rent or anything – Kip's dad could get in trouble.'

'*And* you're putting kids in danger,' added Kip. 'That last film we went into? What with the bullets, the sharks, the erupting volcano and everything else . . . well, I don't think the police are going to clap their hands and say "well done" if news of that gets out. That's assuming anybody believes it.'

'Oh dear,' said Mr Lazarus bleakly. He sighed and looked as though he might be about to burst into tears. 'And then there's Dario to consider. Once he finds me, he just keeps on and on, pushing, probing, trying to get me to go along with his latest scheme . . .' He shook his head. 'It's no good,' he said. 'I was hoping it wouldn't come to this, but . . . I'm afraid I'm going to have to consider moving on.'

Kip and Beth exchanged looks of alarm.

'Moving on?' said Beth. 'What do you mean?'

'I mean I might have to leave.'

'You can't do that!' said Kip.

'I really don't see that I have any other choice.'

'But . . . what about the Paramount? We've only just got it going properly. It's been going downhill for years and you've changed all that. You . . . you can't just walk away from it.'

'I might have no other option,' said Mr Lazarus. 'Oh, Kip, don't look at me like that! You surely don't imagine this is the first time this has happened? Yours is not the only cinema I have helped.'

'That's not the point,' said Beth. 'Kip's dad is depending on you. We *all* are.'

'I know, my dear. And please don't think it's something I *want* to do. But if everything is going to blow up in my face, I really don't want to be here when it happens. You surely can't blame me for that?'

'Let's not panic,' said Kip. 'There must be something we can do.'

'There is,' said Beth in her calm, confident way and, as she talked, Kip knew exactly why he chose to hang out with her. 'Here's what we do. Mr L, you tell Kip's dad that you're in the process of moving house. You had a big row with your landlord and you just walked out of there.'

Mr Lazarus looked shocked. 'Why exactly did I do that?' he asked.

'Because . . . you had a leaky roof and the landlord wouldn't do anything about it.'

'I see . . .'

'Then we find you a flat.'

'A flat?'

'Yes, somewhere in the village. There are plenty of little apartments for rent, I always see the signs. It's just a case of calling in to one of the estate agents and looking at a couple of properties. You can do that, you're free most days.'

'But . . . what about my equipment? The Enigma? I can't leave it unguarded overnight.'

'You won't have to. You won't actually be *living* in the flat, will you?'

Mr Lazarus looked bemused. 'I won't?'

'No. But you'll have a real address, somewhere to get mail delivered, stuff like that. You'll just have to pop in from time to time and make sure it's OK. Maybe store a few of your things there. That should keep Mr McCall off your back.'

Mr Lazarus frowned. 'And how much is a place like that going to cost me?'

Beth waved a hand as if it was of no importance. 'You can go for the smallest, cheapest bug hutch you can find. It doesn't matter. And Mr McCall *does* pay you, doesn't he? It'll be worth spending the money for the peace of mind you'll have. The other thing...'

'Yes?' said Mr Lazarus apprehensively.

'The other thing' – Beth looked stern – 'is you'll have to stop sending people into films.'

'Oh, but—'

'No buts, Mr L. It has to stop. Yes, I know, it's incredible, fantastic, amazing, all that stuff... and I'll never forget the things that happened to me in those movies. But it's too risky and if it ever got out that you were sending kids into films, you'd end up in the worst kind of trouble. They might even put you in jail.'

'Jail? Could they *do* such a thing?'

'It happens,' said Kip, as though he had personal experience of it.

'So,' continued Beth, 'you'll have to tell your collector friends that it's over with. No more trips into the movies to pick up props.'

Mr Lazarus sighed. He seemed to be thinking it through. 'I'll still have to go in myself occasionally,' he said. 'Just into my own little piece of film, to keep myself looking young. Dario too, for that matter, I can't deny him the occasional top-up.'

Beth shrugged. 'That's different,' she said. 'What you and Dario get up to is your own business. But no more sending kids in, Mr L. Deal?'

Mr Lazarus nodded. 'Deal,' he said. 'And... Dario?'

'You'll just have to put your foot down,' she said, though she looked less certain now. 'Tell him you're not going to let him push you around. Tell him he's just your kid brother and he has to behave himself.'

Mr Lazarus chuckled. 'If only it were as easy as that,' he said. 'But, yes, I'll tell him the very next time I see him.'

Kip let out a long breath. It looked as though disaster had been averted, at least for the time being. He felt like hugging Beth, but thought he'd wait until they were alone.

'Great,' he said. 'So, we'll get working on all that. And that should sort everything out, right? We can go on as we were?'

There was a silence and then Mr Lazarus nodded. 'I expect so,' he said.

'Great,' he repeated. 'All we have to do now is

make the launch a night to remember.' He lifted his mug of coffee. 'To *Space Blasters*!'

Beth and Mr Lazarus raised their own mugs and the three of them drank to its success.

Chapter Six

The Big Night

The big night had finally arrived. Dad was already up at the cinema, handling the last-minute details. Things looked promising. Over eighty tickets had already been pre-booked, an occurrence that was completely unknown in Kip's experience. At the Paramount, punters generally just turned up and paid on the night.

The previous evening, an important detail had dropped into place. The full-page piece in the *Evening Post* had appeared under the title **KIP HAS A BLAST!** Stephanie's article gave the impression that it was Kip who actually managed the cinema and that Dad was just his helper. Kip was outraged by this, but Dad said it didn't matter what Stephanie *said*, what was important was the free publicity. Mr Lazarus had ended up with nothing more than a brief mention, saying that 'cinema projectionist Mr Lazarus has had a long and varied career in the cinema and previously worked at Il Cappuccino in

Venice.' Kip thought that this made it sound like he'd been a waiter in a coffee bar, but at least it wasn't delving too deeply into things that would be better left alone. Mr L must have done a better job of putting her off the scent than he'd thought.

There had been a bit of bad news as well though. Dad had got a call in the afternoon from somebody who claimed to be Sally Lovely's agent, announcing that the *Corporation Road* star would be unable to attend the premier due to 'work commitments' but wishing them every success with their venture. This was a bit awkward, as Dad had announced in the article that there'd be a special mystery guest star. 'I suppose we'll just have to wheel out Norman,' he said. Norman was the Paramount's previous projectionist, the man whose retirement had created an opening for Mr Lazarus. He'd phoned earlier in the week announcing his intention to attend the launch with his sister, Kitty.

'He's not exactly famous,' Kip had complained.

'He'll have to do,' Dad had said. 'We don't have time to sort somebody else out, not this late in the game.'

★ ★ ★

Kip and Beth walked down the road to the cinema trying to rein in their mounting excitement. They were both surprised and delighted to see that there was already a sizeable queue forming outside the swing doors. As they reached the steps, the doors opened and two white armour-clad space troopers walked out and took up positions on either side of the entrance, realistic laser rifles at the ready.

'Wow,' said Kip. 'Cool.' He and Beth climbed the steps towards the doors but one of the space troopers stepped forward and placed a gloved hand on his chest. 'Hold on, sunshine,' he growled from behind his smoked glass visor. 'Where d'ya fink you're going?'

'Into the cinema,' said Kip, waving a hand at the door.

The other trooper came forward to stand with his friend. 'Perhaps you didn't notice,' he said, pointing down the steps, 'there's a queue.'

'Oh . . . don't worry, my dad owns the Paramount,' explained Kip nervously. They did look terrifying even though he knew it was only fancy dress. 'We're here to help him out.'

'Yeah and I'm Mary Poppins,' said the space trooper. 'Get to the back of the queue.'

'He's telling the truth!' cried Beth. 'He's Kip McCall, his dad really does own this place.'

'Yeah,' said the first space trooper. 'And if I had a fiver for every kid who's tried that one, I'd be a millionaire.'

Luckily, just at that moment, the door opened and Dad came out, dragging a reluctant Mr Lazarus with him. They were accompanied by Stephanie Holder, who was carrying an expensive-looking camera.

'Ah, Kip, Beth,' said Dad. 'Good timing. What do you think of our space troopers?'

'I think they take their work a bit too seriously,' muttered Beth, but Dad didn't seem to notice. 'Beth, this is Stephanie from the *Evening Post*. Did you see her article about us yesterday? She's already planning a follow-up piece for next week,' he explained.

'This is the biggest thing that's happened in the village in ages,' said Stephanie. 'And when I started doing a little reading about Mr Lazarus's career, I realised there was more of a story here than I'd originally thought.'

'Really?' croaked Mr Lazarus.

'Oh, yes,' said Stephanie, giving him an odd look. 'You're a very interesting man and I think our readers would like to know all about you. Now, let's get a picture of you with the space troopers, shall we?'

'I really should get inside,' said Mr Lazarus. 'I need to check the equipment.'

'You've plenty of time for that,' Dad assured him. 'There's half an hour before the doors open. Come on, we need a shot of Team Paramount.'

'But I haven't shaved this morning,' groaned Mr Lazarus.

'Nonsense, you look fine.' Dad pushed everyone into position, and the space troopers – clearly well practised at this sort of thing – stood at either side of the group with their rifles trained on them, as though taking them hostage. Stephanie shuffled a few steps back and lifted her camera. 'Say gorgonzola!'

They did as she instructed and she fired off what sounded like a whole volley of shots.

'Whoops,' she said. 'Not really used to this fancy camera, I borrowed it from Bob, our regular photographer. Now, what about getting one of the mystery guest?'

'Er . . . he's not here yet,' said Dad. 'I'll give you a shout when he arrives.'

'He?' Stephanie seemed disappointed. 'I heard it was going to be Sally Lovely.'

'Don't know where you got that idea from,' said Dad, heading back towards the entrance. 'Come on, everyone, let's get cracking.' He nodded to the space troopers. 'Once you've got the queue inside, you guys can find the seats I reserved for you.'

'They're watching the movie?' murmured Kip.

'Yes,' said Dad. He lowered his voice. 'It reduced their fee by quite a bit,' he added and winked. 'Right, in we go!'

Kip, Beth and Mr Lazarus followed him inside and left Stephanie snapping more pictures of the space troopers. Kip couldn't quite resist giving them a satisfied smirk as he went by.

Once inside, Dad started giving orders. 'Mr L, now's the time to do that last-minute check. Kip, Beth . . . you know what to do. From the way that queue's forming, I'd say we're going to be even busier than we'd thought.'

Mr Lazarus hurried into the auditorium and Kip and Beth took up their positions in the confectionary booth. Kip suddenly thought of something as he switched on the popcorn machine. 'Dad,' he said.

'Yes?'

'I know we're busy and everything, but . . . you haven't forgotten it's a Friday night, have you?'

'Don't worry. I've put reserved stickers on three seats in the front row,' he said. 'When the trailers start, you can slip in there and take your places.'

'Three?'

'Yes. Rose is coming too, remember?'

'Oh, yeah.' Kip tried not to look too annoyed. 'Is Mum not going to be here?'

Dad sighed and shook his head. 'I thought tonight, for once, I might persuade her to pop along,' he said. 'But you know her. She'd rather be boiled in oil than have to sit through something like *Space Blasters*.'

Kip nodded. He'd never understood why Mum seemed so uninterested in movies. Dad had tried hard over the years to persuade her to join in, but had got nowhere. Ah, well, he thought, it was her loss. He grabbed a large bag of corn kernels and upended them into the machine. 'How much shall I make?' he asked.

'Just keep it coming,' Dad advised him.

Dad was right. The Paramount was packed. By the time the doors opened, the queue stretched halfway down the high street, and more and more people seemed to be arriving all the time. Kip and Beth were kept very busy, dispensing popcorn and soft drinks and toffees and ice creams, while in the office Dad was selling tickets as fast as he could tear them off the strip. He'd taken the precaution of only allowing as many tickets as he actually had seats for, not a problem he'd ever had to consider before – but it began to look as though it had been a wise move.

Norman came in and picked up his complimentary tickets, and then he and his sister took their places in the queue for confectionery. 'Norman!' said Kip in as cheerful a voice as he could manage. 'Great to see you. And this must be...Kitty.' It would have been hard to imagine anybody less suited to the name, or less like Kitty Velour, the beautiful special agent Kip had met in *Spy Another Day*. *This* Kitty was a huge woman in a tatty fur coat and a battered felt hat. She had a face like a WWE wrestler. 'Pleased to meet you,' she growled, reaching out a hand the size of a ham and nearly crushing Kip's fingers to pulp.

'Er...hi,' said Kip, trying not to wince.

'I can't believe what you've done with the old

place,' said Norman, gazing around in awe. 'It . . . it's like a different cinema entirely.'

'It's not bad, is it?' said Kip proudly. 'You remember Beth?'

'I do. You two still courting strong?' Kip felt his cheeks burning and he saw Beth suppress a smirk.

'Er . . . what can I get for you?' asked Kip.

'Two Cokes and a large bag of Maltesers,' said Norman. Kip and Beth handed the items across and Norman and Kitty promptly walked off without paying for them.

'Some things don't change,' murmured Kip irritably. He glanced at Beth. 'What are you smiling at?' he asked.

'Courting strong,' she giggled. 'I've never heard it called *that* before.'

Kip was about to reply when something caught his eye. Amongst the lively press of people in the foyer, he caught a brief glimpse of a fat figure, dressed in a leather jacket, pushing his way through the doors of the gents. It looked a bit like Dario. Kip hoped that, if it *were* him, he hadn't come here to cause trouble. Kip already had his work cut out keeping an eye on Stephanie, who seemed to be popping up all over the place and snapping photographs, as though doing her best to snoop. And what had she meant by that remark about the reading she'd done on Mr Lazarus?

Then Rose appeared at the head of the queue. Mum must have dropped her off at the entrance and sent her inside. As usual, she demanded half her own weight in sweets. Kip began sorting them out for her and Dario slipped from his mind. As he turned back to face Rose, she lifted her birthday-present mobile phone and snapped a picture of him. He scowled at her. 'What's that in aid of?' he asked her. The phone was now never out of her hand and, since she'd got fed up with texting inane messages to her schoolmates, she spent most of her time photographing everyone and everything she saw.

'Daddy told me to take lots of pictures tonight,' said Rose, self-importantly. 'He says if I can get a good one, we might be able to put it in the paper.'

'There's somebody here from the *Evening Post* with a proper camera,' Kip told her. 'And, besides, they won't want one of me.'

'Oh, no, that one's just for my research,' she told him. 'I've got my eye on you.'

'I don't know what you're talking about,' said Kip.

'Yes you do. Something funny is going on. And I'm going to find out what it is.'

He shoved the various packets of food at her. 'Go and take your seat,' he advised. 'And for a change, try not to ask dumb questions all through the film.'

Rose flashed him a challenging look, but she went in through the swing doors of the auditorium.

'Just remember,' whispered Beth. 'She's your little sister. And I seem to remember you promising to be nicer to her a while ago.'

'I know,' said Kip, gritting his teeth. He crumpled an empty paper carton and dropped it in the bin. 'But it's so hard sometimes.'

At a little after eight p.m., Dad sold the last available tickets. There was nothing he could do but herd the twenty or so disappointed people who'd failed to get a seat back to the entrance and suggest that they return the following evening. He locked the doors and scrawled a hasty HOUSE FULL sign, which he taped to the glass. Then he turned to look at Kip and Beth, his face shiny with sweat. He waited until the last couple of punters had gone into the auditorium and then he clapped his hands. 'I don't believe it!' he cried gleefully. 'The last time this happened here was when my dad had *The*

Sound of Music on! That was 1965.' He looked wistful. 'I wish Dad was still alive to see this. He'd have been so proud.'

Kip grinned. 'We've run out of quite a few things here,' he announced. 'You'll have to get a fresh order in for tomorrow.'

'I'll sort all that out,' said Dad. 'Now, you two have worked hard tonight. Grab some of the snacks that are left and get yourselves in there. I'll watch the film another night.' He glanced at his watch. 'It's just about to start.'

Kip and Beth didn't need to be told twice. They helped themselves to drinks and chocs, came out from behind the counter and hurried into the darkened auditorium. As they descended the stairs to the front row, the lights dimmed fully and a familiar theme tune started up in crystal clear stereo. Then those iconic titles began to slide up the screen into the distance. Kip and Beth settled into their seats next to Rose.

'Show time,' whispered Kip.

Chapter Seven

A Problem

Onscreen, a sleek space ship soared through the furthermost reaches of the galaxy. At the controls, young Zeke Stardancer was on the most important mission of his life – an attempt to rescue his fiancée, Princess Shanna, who in the previous film, *Assault of the Skyhawks*, had been taken prisoner by the evil Emperor Zarkan.

Zeke was at the helm of the *Trillenium Hawk* with his trusty Silonian co-pilot, Blutacca, by his side. He was currently making his way through an asteroid belt, swerving and spinning through a maelstrom of hurtling debris and occasionally relying on his laser cannon to blast larger obstacles out of his path.

'Hang on tight, Blooey,' he said through gritted teeth. 'This could get rough. May the power be with us.'

'Who's that?' asked Rose, much too loudly. 'I've never seen *him* before.'

'That's Zeke Stardancer,' hissed Kip. 'And you *have* seen him before. He's in all the films.'

'He wasn't in the last one.'

'Of course he was!'

'No, he wasn't. And what's that thing with him? Looks like a big teddy bear.'

'That's Blutacca. He's a Silonian.'

'A what?'

'A Silonian! A creature from the Planet Silon.'

In the row behind them somebody made a shushing sound.

'Sorry,' muttered Kip.

A large asteroid caught Zeke's ship a glancing blow and the audience drew in a collective breath, as the Lazarus Enigma made each and every one of them feel the impact of the collision. The *Trillenium Hawk* lurched to one side and Zeke and Blooey were thrown about in their seats . . . but at that moment the image cut to a long shot, revealing that a dark, bat-shaped star fighter was rapidly closing in on them.

The scene cut briefly to its pilot, a Draconian, one of the lizard-men mercenaries who fought for the Emperor. He was wearing a distinctive black jumpsuit decorated with blood-red insignia and a pair of yellow goggles. He smiled coldly and a forked tongue flicked briefly in and out of his scaly mouth. His claw-like hand edged towards the firing button on his laser cannon . . .

Just at that moment, back in the real world, somebody came in through the entrance doors of the auditorium, allowing them to swing shut with a loud bump. Kip glanced over his shoulder in irritation and noticed a fat figure waddling through the entrance. It was Dario, Kip was sure of it now. Had he been waiting in the gents' toilets all this time? As Kip stared, Dario swung round drunkenly and, weaving from side to side, started lurching up the stairs at the back of the auditorium, heading towards the projection room.

Kip was torn. He wanted to watch the film, of course he did, but there was something about Dario's swaying figure that spoke of trouble. Dad couldn't afford to have anything go wrong tonight. So reluctantly Kip leaned close to Beth, whispered 'Back in a minute,' and got out of his seat. He followed Dario up the stairs, picking his way with difficulty in the semi-darkness. Behind him on the screen, an action set piece was unfolding and the eyes of everyone in the audience were fixed to it.

Nobody seemed to notice Kip as he moved up the aisle, even the various friends from his school who were here tonight.

As he neared the projection room, he became aware of the sound of raised voices from within – and then, more alarmingly, a loud thump as something fell to the ground. Kip quickened his pace. He reached the door, pushed it open and stepped inside, closing it behind him in an attempt to contain the sound. What he saw in there startled him.

Mr Lazarus and Dario were locked together in a violent tussle. Dario had his arms around Mr Lazarus's neck and the brothers were flailing about inside the cramped room like a couple of kids fighting in a school playground. They reeled sideways against a workbench and an old camera rolled off and hit the ground with a crunch.

'Hey, stop this!' yelled Kip, running forward, but even as he did so, the two men lurched backwards towards the projector, through which the roll of film was currently clattering. For a moment, it looked as though they were going to crash into it, and Kip steeled himself for the impact, but at the last instant, Dario tripped and they veered slightly to one side, heading instead towards the Lazarus Enigma. Kip could see what was about to happen and he tried to make a frantic grab for them. He was too late. Mr Lazarus's legs gave out from under him and the two men fell, still struggling, onto the wooden platform, their impetus launching it forward on its well-oiled wheels. An instant later, the two grappling figures slid into the pool of brilliant light reflected down from the prism. They shimmered for an instant and then they were gone.

Kip stood there, staring open-mouthed at the empty platform. 'Oh no,' he whispered. Seconds later, he heard a collected gasp of astonishment from the cinema audience. He ran to the viewing window and looked at the screen.

The two men had timed their entrance into the film very badly. An instant earlier, they'd have been in the rocket ship with the good guys, Zeke and Blutacca. But the film had just cut back to the Draconian starfighter and now Mr Lazarus and Dario were rolling about on the cockpit floor behind a rather startled lizard-man pilot. He glanced over his shoulder, furious that he'd been put off his aim and shouted for his two companions to grab the newcomers who had literally just appeared out of thin air. The Draconians unstrapped themselves from their seats and ran to grab the struggling humans, who still hadn't realised that they were no longer in the projection room. They were pulled roughly apart and their arms pinned behind their backs. Mr Lazarus finally realised that something was amiss. He turned to look out from the cinema screen, his startled face in extreme close up.

Then he said something very rude, something that Kip didn't quite catch but, whatever it was, it certainly wasn't the kind of thing you'd expect to hear in a *Space Blasters* movie. A wave of laughter rippled through the audience, together with a few gasps from outraged parents and Kip realised that this was a potential disaster. He had to do something about it. Now the Draconians were dragging Mr Lazarus and Dario through a hatchway, allowing the pilot to go back to his task of blowing the *Trillenium Hawk* to bits.

Kip felt like pulling out his hair and was only grateful that Dad was still down in the ticket office, missing this. But what if he came in later on to have a look? As Kip stared nonplussed at the screen, he noticed somebody hurrying up the steps towards him. Beth. An instant later, the door swung open and she burst into the projection room. 'M . . . M . . .

Mr Lazarus!' she stammered, jerking a thumb over her shoulder. 'He's . . . he's in the bloody MOVIE!'

'I know.' Kip shook his head. 'He was fighting with Dario. They fell and . . .'

He broke off as he noticed another figure standing in the open doorway, her hands on her hips and an indignant expression on her face. Rose. She must have followed Beth up the stairs. 'What's going on?' she demanded.

'Nothing!' said Kip, rather too quickly. He stepped forward, grabbed his little sister's wrist and pulled her into the room, closing the door behind her.

'I just saw Mr Lazarus in the film,' she said.

'No,' said Kip. 'No, it wasn't him. Just . . . somebody who *looked* like him.'

Rose looked around the narrow confines of the projection room. 'Where is he then?' she demanded. 'Why isn't he in here showing the film?'

'He . . . he just popped outside for a bit,' said Kip, desperately.

'Right. I'm telling Dad,' said Rose, turning back towards the door.

'NO!' Kip lunged past her and barred her way. 'You can't tell him, he'll only . . . worry.'

'It's *his* cinema,' said Rose. 'Something weird is going on and he needs to know about it.'

'He doesn't,' said Beth a little more calmly. 'Trust us on this, Rose. If he finds out, he's likely to go mental.'

Rose seemed to consider for a moment whether this would be a bad thing or not. 'Well, how did Mr Lazarus get *in* the film?' she asked.

But Kip had already turned away and was rooting through the jumble of equipment on the worktop.

'What are you doing?' asked Beth warily.

'What do you think I'm doing?' muttered Kip, deciding that things were too out of control to keep lying in front of his sister. 'He's gone in there without the Retriever, hasn't he? I'll have to follow him and bring him out again.'

'Kip, no. Remember what we said? It's too dangerous in there.'

'What else can we do?' asked Kip. 'We can't leave him, can we? Those Draconians are really nasty, they'll probably. . . kill him.'

'They'll probably kill you,' Beth reminded him. 'We said we'd never go in there again.'

'I know what we said,' snapped Kip, searching through the litter of stuff on the worktop. 'But we have to get him back. Otherwise he'll be trapped in there for ever. Then what happens to the Paramount?' His fingers closed on the Retriever – an oval lump of Perspex on a length of chain with a hinged metal cover across the front of it. He snapped open the cover to ensure that the device was pulsing with a dull red glow. He closed it again and hung the Retriever around his neck. Now he was looking for the tiny earpiece that he had worn when he'd gone into a film before – the device that allowed him to keep in touch with somebody in the projection room. He found two of them, pushed one into his right ear and handed the other to Beth.

'You'll have to stay here and direct operations,' he said.

She shook her head. 'No way, Jose. If you're going in, I'm coming with you.'

Kip glared at her. 'Beth, we don't have time to argue about this. I've got less than two hours to get Mr L back. I need you to stay here and talk me through this.'

'But . . .'

'Please, just do it,' he begged her.

'You're going into the film?' cried Rose. She

turned back towards the door. 'Right! I *am* telling Dad,' she said.

'No!' cried Beth. She grabbed Rose's hand. 'Just hang on a moment, I'll explain everything to you in a minute.' She glanced at Kip and pushed the second earpiece into her own ear. 'You'd better take care in there,' she told him.

'I will,' he promised her. 'Don't worry.' He turned away and pulled the wooden platform out of the light to the end of its track. Then he placed one foot on it. Beth moved to the viewing window.

'You've got to be careful how you time this,' she warned him. 'The cameras keep cutting between the two space ships. Which one do you want to be on?

'The Draconian ship, of course,' said Kip, trying to sound a lot more confident that he actually felt. 'The one Mr L and Dario are on. With any luck, I can just grab them and hit the eject button.'

'What you don't want is to hit a scene when the camera is doing a long shot,' said Beth. 'If that happens, you'll be outside both ships in outer space and then . . .'

'Then what?'

'Well . . . you won't be able to breathe.'

Kip swallowed hard. 'Good point,' he said. 'Well,

that's why I need you here. To guide me.' He took up his starting position. 'Tell me when to go,' he murmured.

'Maybe you should wait until we get to a calmer scene?'

'There isn't time,' said Kip. 'I've got to get in there quick, before the Draconians do something drastic to Mr L. Count me in.'

'OK. Kip? I love you.'

'What?'

'I . . .'

'I heard what you said, Beth, but this isn't the best time.'

'Well, you might at least say it back!'

'Beth . . .'

'You may not get another chance.'

'All right, I love you! Now can we please do this thing?'

'Sure. Ready?'

'Ready as I'll ever be.'

Beth's gaze was fixed on the frantic action onscreen. She was waiting for the camera to cut back to the Federation ship.

'Goodbye, Kip,' said Rose gravely. 'Try not to do anything silly while you're in there.'

'Silly?' Kip stared at her. 'Like what?'

But there was no time for Rose to answer, as Beth gave the instructions. 'OK, I think we can... yes, ready... steady... GO!'

Kip pushed off hard with his left foot and the wooden platform shot forward into the light – but even as he went, he heard Beth shout the word 'WAIT!' Too late. His entire body felt as though it was melting and then he was falling into the light, spinning around like a leaf in a hurricane. He came abruptly back to his senses and sat there, staring around in dismay.

He was sitting on something soft and furry. Glancing up, he saw a baffled beastly face glaring down at him.

'Snargle ela thrump gat?' grunted Blutacca, which was probably Silonian for, 'Why are you sitting in my lap?'

Kip turned his head to the side and saw the pilot of the *Trillenium Hawk* staring at him in utter amazement.

'By the flaming moons of Heera, where did you come from, boy?' cried Zeke Stardancer.

CHAPTER EIGHT
All Aboard

Kip opened his mouth to reply and in the same instant, Blutacca whipped a laser pistol from the holster on his furry hip and held it to the side of Kip's head. 'Trontle diggle enthwip?' he growled.

'Not just yet, Blooey,' said Zeke. He studied Kip for a moment. 'He just asked me if he should shoot you,' he explained.

'Oh,' agreed Kip. 'I figured that's what it was.'

'You speak Silonian?'

'Er... no, it was more of a guess.'

'I'm so sorry,' whispered Beth's voice in Kip's right ear. 'The cameras cut away just at the last moment. I tried to warn you.'

Kip nodded, very carefully, just in case the movement caused Blutacca's finger to tighten on the trigger. Then he turned his head to look ahead through the cockpit screen and noticed that a huge asteroid was hurtling straight towards them. 'Er...' he said. 'I think—'

'Fear not.' Zeke casually hit the fire button and the asteroid exploded into a million fragments. A few moments later, a myriad of tiny pieces of rock were bouncing off the screen.

'That was close,' hissed Beth's voice in Kip's ear.

'Now,' said Zeke, calmly. His deep blue eyes studied Kip from beneath a fringe of shaggy blond hair. 'What do you think I should tell Blooey?'

'Tell him not to fire,' gasped Kip. 'Tell him I'm on your side.'

Zeke looked doubtful. 'And how do I know that's the case?' he asked. 'I've never laid eyes on you before. Who are you, young traveller? And how in the name of Saturn's rings did you get here?'

'I'm Kip McCall. And I was . . . sent here to . . . to help you.'

'Sent here by whom?'

'By . . . by Mardy Windoid of the Rebel Alliance,' said Kip, picking a *Space Blasters* character at random from the extensive memory bank in his head.

'And what planet are you from?'

'I'm from Earth. But I joined the Alliance a few months ago. I wanted to help you to defeat the Emperor Zarkan.'

'A noble aim. And how old are you?'

'I'm nearly fourteen,' said Kip.

Zeke smiled. 'That is the age I was when I first joined up,' he said. 'A young boy on the very cusp of manhood.'

'Right! So er… Mardy sent me here to warn you about something.'

'Oh, really? What's that?'

'There's a Draconian starfighter on your tail and it's about to blow you to bits!'

Zeke's eyes narrowed. He hit a switch on the control panel in front of him and a red light began to flash on and off on his display. He glanced accusingly at Blutacca. 'Thundering asteroids, Blooey, he's right! How is it that you didn't pick it up on your sensors?'

Blutacca grunted. Then he brought a huge fist down on the dashboard and a red light began to blink on his screen too.

'Yarlf narra toogle scredge folp,' he said, which probably translated as something like, 'Wait till I have a word with those IT people.'

Zeke nodded. He flashed a pearly white grin at Kip. 'I appreciate your timely warning, youngster. Blooey, engage rear laser cannon. We'll let those scaly vermin get a little closer and then we'll blast them out of existence.'

'Oh, but you can't!' cried Kip.

Zeke looked disappointed. 'Why not?' he muttered.

'There's . . . there's somebody on board. A friend of mine. A good friend of Mardy's too. The Draconians have taken him prisoner.'

Zeke shrugged. 'What's that to me?' he asked.

'Well it's Mr . . .' Kip hesitated, not wanting to give the real name. 'It's Mr Barty Skythump,' he said, making up a name that he thought sounded right for the film.

'Who?'

'Mr Barty Skythump. Of the . . . the Rebel Alliance. And . . . without him . . .'

'Yes?'

Kip's mind raced as he tried to think of a convincing argument.

'Princess Shanna?' murmured Beth's voice in his ear.

'Yes! Without him, you'll never be able to find Princess Shanna!'

This made Zeke sit up and take notice, though he continued to steer the spaceship expertly through the oncoming space debris at the same time. 'What do you know about her?' he muttered.

Plenty, thought Kip. After all, he had five earlier films to draw on, not to mention a whole library of books and comics on the subject back home in his bedroom. 'Let me see now... She was born on the planet Enterrium Two. She has a brother called Genrod and a sister called Luanna. She's... she's due to inherit the throne of Lippidisimus on her eighteenth birthday, but she was abducted by Emperor Zarkan, at the end of the last fi— The last... recently.'

Zeke looked impressed. 'I've been searching the galaxy, hoping to find some trace of her,' he said. 'Do you know where she is being held captive?'

'Er... no, but... Mr Skythump does. That's why the Draconians have kidnapped him, see? To shut him up. So it would be mental to blow up that ship.'

'Hmm.' Zeke frowned. 'I do not understand this word, "mental."'

'Umm. It would be... unwise,' said Kip, trying to speak like a character from these films would. 'The... the omens would not be good.'

Zeke nodded gravely. 'There is wisdom in what you say. I cannot very well blow up a ship in which such an important ally is travelling. But neither can

I remain here like a sitting snood-fowl. What would you advise, Blooey?'

'Arggh snelter gromple thudda shoo,' said Blutacca, which probably meant something like, 'I'm not paid to make those kind of decisions!'

Kip thought for a moment. 'You could try something sneaky,' he suggested.

'Go on,' said Zeke.

'You could send out your inner cloak to shield the back of the *Trillenium Hawk* and pretend to take a hit from the Draconian ship. Then you could put out a cloud of engine smoke and veer away, as though the ship is out of control ...'

'Yes?'

'Well, *then* you could hide behind a planetoid and when the enemy ship goes by, you could follow at a safe distance.'

Zeke's jaw dropped. 'That's incredible,' he said. 'You think just like I do. I did something like that once before.'

Yes, thought Kip. *In the last movie. It worked that time.*

'But ... why should I follow them?'

'Because ... because ...' Kip couldn't really think of a good reason. Luckily, Beth whispered into his

84

ear and he just parroted what she said.

'Because they'll go straight to Emperor Zarkan to report that they've shot you down. And wherever Zarkan is, *that's* where Princess Shanna will be.'

'Brilliant!' said Zeke and he slammed the flat of his hand down on the dashboard. 'Little wonder that Mardy has such high regard for you! It shall be so. Blooey, put the pistol away and take over the controls.'

Blutacca swung into action. With one huge hand, he swept Kip off his lap and then concentrated on steering the spaceship through the asteroid storm. Meanwhile, Zeke sat back in his seat and closed his eyes. Kip knew exactly what he was doing. He was summoning his inner cloak and sending it out as an invisible force field to protect the rear of the ship. The 'cloak' was a fairly new thing. Zeke had only discovered he had this power in the last film, when the tiny mystic shaman, Scoda, had taught him how to harness it and use it to his advantage. Scoda was a two-foot-high green creature with pointed ears and a very odd way of talking. He was also pretty handy with a laser sword. Or to put it in his way of speaking, pretty handy with a laser sword he was.

Meanwhile, on the screen in front of Kip, the blinking red dot that was the Draconian starfighter was rapidly converging on the blinking green dot that was the *Trillenium Hawk*.

★ ★ ★

The Draconians flung Mr Lazarus and Dario into a square windowless room, somewhere down in the bowels of the ship. They left and one of them placed a scaly hand on a sensor on the far wall. A series of metal rods moved silently sideways to bar the entrance. The Draconians muttered a few indecipherable words to each other and then strode away. Mr Lazarus looked hopefully around the room, seeking some avenue of escape. It was completely bare apart from a narrow bunk jutting out from one wall. He walked across to it and sat down heavily. Then he looked despairingly at the fat figure of his brother who lay slumped on the floor, breathing hard. He was red in the face and, even from this distance, Mr Lazarus could smell the alcohol on him.

'Well,' said Mr Lazarus, 'here's another nice mess you've gotten me into.'

Dario looked up at him in befuddled amazement. 'Where are we?' he muttered.

'Where do you suppose we are? We fell onto the Enigma platform when we were fighting. We're in *Space Blasters.*'

Dario sat up and stared round. He seemed to be thinking hard about this. 'Is there likely to be any treasure in this film?' he asked.

Mr Lazarus glared at his brother. 'Is that all you can think about? Your damned get-rich-quick schemes? Don't you realise what you've done? We're trapped in here. And I don't have the Retriever with me.'

Dario struggled back to his feet and stumbled across to sit down beside his brother. 'What, that funny gadget you always hang around my neck when I go into the *Elixir of Youth*?'

'Yes, *that*,' snarled Mr Lazarus. 'Without it, we can't leave the film.'

Dario shook his head. 'Well, that was pretty dumb,' he said.

'Dumb?' Mr Lazarus glared at him incredulously.

'Yes, if it's that important, you should have it with you at all times. That's what *I* would do.'

'Would you, indeed?' Mr Lazarus was resisting a

powerful impulse to punch his brother on the nose. 'So now you're saying it's my fault this happened?'

Dario shrugged. 'You should be prepared for any eventuality,' he said. 'Only an idiot would not be.'

'I'll tell you what I wasn't prepared for,' said Mr Lazarus. 'My stupid brother, turning up drunk out of his mind and starting a fight on the night of a big film launch. Have you any idea of the damage you have done?'

'Well, I . . .'

'Not only are we stuck in this lousy cell in this lousy film, but also our entry to it will have been witnessed by a whole cinema full of people. What do you suppose they're thinking now, eh?'

Dario smiled. 'Mama always said I should have been a movie star,' he said. He looked around. 'Where do you suppose the cameras are?'

Mr Lazarus shook his head. 'Oh, don't deceive yourself. Nobody is interested in what we're doing. We're just bit-players in this story. And if you don't mind, I'd prefer it if you left our mother out of this.'

Dario looked disappointed. 'What's the problem?' he asked. 'You never like talking about Mama. Is it because I was always her favourite?'

Mr Lazarus laughed at that. 'Now I know you are deluded!' he said. 'You weren't her favourite; you were the thorn in her side. She never slept at night for worrying about you.'

'Mama loved me,' Dario assured him. 'When she made spaghetti, I always got the biggest portion.' He slapped his big belly contentedly. 'But never mind bickering. We're in the film. The question is, how do we get out of it?'

'We have only one hope,' said Mr Lazarus.

'Which is?'

'That young Kip takes pity on us and comes into the film with the Retriever.'

'Kip? The boy I saw the other day?'

Mr Lazarus nodded. 'That's the one,' he said.

'If he's a real friend of yours, then he's certain to come,' reasoned Dario.

'I'm not so sure. He was only telling me recently how he never wanted to enter a film again. And the only thing I can say to him is that, if he'll do it just this once more, I promise...' He raised his voice on the off-chance that Kip might somehow be able to see or hear him. 'I swear on my Enigma... that I'll never ask him to do it again.' He paused and waited, hoping against hope that Kip might suddenly appear beside him, but nothing happened. He sighed. 'I don't think he'll do it.'

'So . . . what do we do now?' asked Dario.

'We just sit here and wait,' said Mr Lazarus. And they settled down to do exactly that.

CHAPTER NINE

Sudden Impact

On the screen, the Draconian pilot narrowed his eyes and lifted his hand back to the fire button. The *Trillenium Hawk* was just emerging from the outer reaches of the meteor storm into open space. In the projection room, Beth and Rose peered through the viewing window, hardly daring to breathe. 'Kip,' murmured Beth. 'The evil ship's getting ready to fire at you.'

There was no answer, but Beth thought she was aware of her boyfriend's soft breathing at the other end of the connection.

'If you can't speak right now, cough to let me know you can hear me.'

There was a short pause and then what sounded more like a sneeze.

'Blud thwip,' said Blutacca's voice. Which might have meant, 'Bless you!'

The image cut to a long shot, showing the two spaceships, now very close to each other.

Suddenly, a burst of laser light shot out from the Draconian star fighter and the rear of the *Trillenium Hawk* exploded in a burst of orange fire. Beth and Rose gasped in horror as the mighty spaceship veered to one side and began to spiral wildly away, a great pall of grey smoke spilling from its fuselage.

'Kip!' cried Beth. 'Kip, are you OK? Please, let me know you're not hurt!' Of course, she had just seen Kip explaining to Zeke how they could fake an explosion, but what was up there onscreen seemed too realistic to be a mere trick.

'What are they doing?' cried Rose. 'If they hurt my brother, I'll . . . I'll smash their faces in! Why can't we *see* him?'

'Because they're doing a long shot. We need to—' Beth broke off as she heard Kip's voice in her ear, sounding strangely formal. 'This seems to be working, Blooey,' he said. 'Those Federation bullies can have no idea that we're completely unharmed.'

'Oodle tango snargle thromp?' said Blutacca, sounding puzzled. It probably meant, 'Why are you telling me this?'

'Everything's all right,' Beth assured Rose. 'I can hear Kip talking. It *was* just the trick they planned.'

'Lucky for the bad guys,' said Rose quietly. Her little hands were bunched into fists and she actually managed to look quite menacing. 'If I have to go in there, they'll be very sorry.'

'I'm sure it won't come to that,' said Beth. Then Zeke's voice spoke in her ear, sounding slightly fuddled. 'How did we do?'

'Zeke, you're back!' said Kip. 'I think it worked.'

'Excellent. Blooey, now plot us a course towards a decent-sized planetoid . . . but take care to make it appear that we're completely out of control.'

Beth gave a sigh of relief. 'It's all good,' she said. 'This is exactly what Kip wanted. If it goes to plan, he should be able to follow the ship Mr Lazarus is on and get him back.'

'I don't know why he's bothering,' said Rose grumpily. 'If it were up to me, I'd leave that creepy old man in the film for ever.'

Beth looked down at Rose with interest. She reached into her ear and took out the communicator, then covered it with her hand so Kip wouldn't hear what was being said.

'Why don't you like Mr Lazarus?' she asked. 'He's really helped out your dad with the cinema and everything.'

Rose scowled. 'Yes, but Kip spends all his time with him and he never wants to play with me any more.'

Beth tried not to smile. So that was it. The old green-eyed monster. 'He *is* a boy,' she pointed out. 'And quite a bit older than you. So he's not really going to want to play the kind of games you like. It doesn't mean he doesn't care about you.'

Rose seemed unconvinced. 'He could still try a bit harder,' she complained. 'I mean, how old is Mr Lazarus, anyway? He must be . . . fifty.'

If only you knew, thought Beth. 'Mr Lazarus is a walking encyclopaedia of cinema,' she said. 'And you know Kip has always been mad about films. So it makes sense they'd be friends.'

Rose looked questioningly up at Beth. 'Have *I* ever been in a film?' she asked.

Beth couldn't bring herself to look Rose in the face. Instead, she kept her eyes fixed on the screen. 'Why do you ask?' she muttered.

'I keep having these dreams,' said Rose. 'About being on an island and there's all these number-tails chasing me . . .'

'Neanderthals,' corrected Beth without thinking, remembering those terrifying creatures on Terror

Island vividly.

'And a helicopter comes and you're in the dream and Kip too. Only... I don't think it *was* a dream, was it?'

Beth sighed and took her eyes away from the screen for a moment. She was worried that Kip might be mad with her for telling Rose the truth, but figured she had no other option. 'No, Rose, it wasn't a dream,' she admitted. 'You remember that film that was on here about a year ago? The one you didn't want to see. *Terror Island*?'

Rose nodded.

'Well, you accidentally ended up in it. You were fooling around in here and you must have somehow stepped onto the Enigma...' She waved a hand at the wooden platform which was still bathed in reflected light. 'Anyway, me and Kip, we went in after you. It was a rescue mission really... just like Kip's doing now.'

'So... if he hadn't come after me...?'

'You'd still be stuck in the film, Rose. You'd never EVER have been able to leave. And of course, when Kip heard that, well... he said to me, "Beth, we have to get her back. She's my little sister and I... well, I love her."'

Rose stared up at Beth, wide-eyed. 'He really said that?' she muttered doubtfully.

'Yes, absolutely. So you see, whatever you think, he *does* care about you.'

Rose nodded. 'Then how come I don't remember being in the film?'

'That was Mr Lazarus's idea,' explained Beth. 'He thought it was all a bit much for somebody so young. So he hypnotised you and tried to make you forget about it. I guess it all came out in your dreams, somehow.'

Rose thought about it for a moment. 'I'm older now,' she said, in case Beth hadn't realised. 'I can handle it.'

'Good.' Beth smiled. 'That's OK then.'

Rose thought for a moment. 'And . . . you know that time when you and Kip were all covered with mud, you smelled of smoke and the soles of Kip's shoes were burned? You'd been into a movie then, hadn't you?'

'Yes, we had,' said Beth, impressed by Rose's powers of deduction. 'We went into a Jason Corder film . . . you know, the spy movies? That was my fault, really. Kip didn't want to do it but I talked him into it. I kind of wanted to meet Daniel Crag.'

Rose's eyes lit up. 'He's *fit*,' she said.

Beth had to smother a laugh. 'Aren't you a bit young to be saying stuff like that?'

'Old enough to know a hunk when I see one,' said Rose.

'Er... yeah, well, he wasn't anything like I expected. And I'll tell you something else that will freak you out. Kip beat him in a fight. Twice!'

'No way,' said Rose.

'Way!' Beth assured her. 'But listen, Rose, all this has to be kept secret, OK? It's between you, me, and Kip. Please don't tell anyone else, not your mum, your dad, not even your bestest friend in the world. If anyone found out, it could mean the end for the Paramount.' She thought for a moment. 'I suppose you could tell Barbie,' she said. 'You could whisper it into her ear. But you must tell her not to pass it on to Ken or one of the other dolls.'

Rose gave her a scornful look. 'How could she?' she asked. 'She's made of plastic.'

'Oh yes,' said Beth, trying not to smile. 'She is, isn't she? I forgot.' She put the communicator back into her ear.

Now Rose craned herself up onto her toes so she

could get a better look at the screen. 'What's happening NOW?' she asked.

★ ★ ★

The *Trillenium Hawk* slid smoothly into the shadow of the planetoid. Looking out of the cockpit, Kip tried not to get too excited. He could see every detail – every crater, every mountain, every blue stretch of water. The planetoid shimmered in a halo of golden light and it looked close enough to reach out and touch, but he knew it was still actually miles away. He was so thrilled to be in a world that he loved so much and, for a moment, all his doubts and fears vanished. He just wanted to enjoy the experience.

Zeke studied his dashboard screen and saw that the flashing red light of the Draconian starship seemed to be moving away from the green light of the *Trillenium Hawk*. 'It appears that our little deception has worked,' he observed. 'They're heading on. Good work, Blooey.'

'Grengethrip,' said Blutacca modestly.

'So all we have to do now,' said Kip, 'is wait until they've gone a little distance and—' He broke off as the cockpit filled with red light and a loud alarm started blaring. 'What's that?' he asked anxiously.

Zeke frowned. He and Blutacca hit some buttons on their respective dashboards and studied them in silence for a few moments. Zeke scowled. 'I'm afraid my cloaking wasn't a hundred per cent successful,' he said. 'We've sustained a little damage to the coolant system.'

'What does that mean?' asked Kip.

'I cannot be certain,' admitted Zeke. 'That's Blooey's area of expertise.' He looked at the Silonian. 'Gelta shabond andro?' he asked.

Blutacca grimaced. 'Eccy thumpo belta swingle,' he said and he pointed towards the planetoid. 'Fara Fawcett tango itchypong!'

Zeke nodded, as though he understood. 'He's saying we'll have to stop somewhere and make a few repairs,' he explained. 'It seems to me that this planetoid is as good a place as any.' He glanced at the screen. 'It's called Tarka Daal,' he observed. He hit a couple more buttons. 'It has a breathable atmosphere and something else we really need to repair the system.'

'What's that?' asked Kip.

'Quanga,' said Blutacca.

'Water,' translated Zeke. He nodded to Blutacca and the Silonian started hitting buttons and flicking switches. The *Trillenium Hawk* moved smoothly forward and started positioning itself for making an orbit of the planetoid.

'But . . . what about the Draconian ship?' cried Kip. 'It's getting away!'

'Calm yourself, young traveller,' Zeke assured him. 'Blooey can programme a following pattern into the onboard computer. It'll lock their co-ordinates into our memory banks. Whether we go after it later today or next week, we'll still know exactly where they've gone.'

'I'd rather not hang around too long,' said Kip nervously. 'I've . . . got things to do.'

'Relax,' Zeke assured him. 'This won't delay us for more than a few hours. It's a fairly simple repair.' He indicated a couple of vacant seats to one side of the fuselage. 'Strap yourself in for the descent,' he said. 'It's a stormy planet and we could be in for a difficult landing.' He seemed to think for a moment. 'Actually, since speed is of the essence, may I call upon you to help us out when we get down there?'

'Kip!' Beth screeched in his ear. 'Tell him no!

You have to come out of the film, what if something happens to you?'

Kip ignored the question even though he knew it probably wasn't a good idea to stay in the film. He'd be better off going back to the projection room and trying to enter the movie in another scene. But he couldn't be sure of meeting up with Mr Lazarus that way and besides, when would he ever get the chance to go on a mission with Zeke Stardancer and Blutacca again? This was an opportunity he couldn't resist. 'What do you need?' he asked Zeke.

'Myself and Blooey will have to work on the actual repairs, but it'd save time if you would fetch the water.'

'What, by myself?' cried Kip.

'Of course not,' said Zeke. 'I would never advise a young traveller to go out on a strange planet without some backup.' He reached to the dashboard and hit a large black button. A door in the fuselage slid silently open and a rattling metal android strode rather jerkily into the room, his head twisting left and right as he came. 'Let me introduce you to T-Twerpio,' said Zeke.

Kip gasped. T-Twerpio was one of his favourite characters.

The android's metal head swivelled in Kip's direction and he spoke in a rasping monotone. 'Goodbye,' he said. 'I'm sad to leave you!'

CHAPTER TEN

T-Twerpio

Kip stared at the android in astonishment. He knew, of course, who T-Twerpio was – he'd featured prominently in every film in the series – but Kip was amazed and excited to see that he was still functioning. He remembered that the android had been blown to bits at the end of the last movie, an event that had caused considerable distress amongst *Space Blasters* fans – including Kip. There had been people talking about it on the internet ever since, some of them even threatening to boycott future films if T-Twerpio were not brought back.

'I didn't think you still had him!' was all Kip could manage to say.

'Oh, he's been through the wars,' admitted Zeke. 'But we've managed to reconstruct him.'

'My mistress has depleted my performance,' explained T-Twerpio. 'She's made me as bad as I will be.'

'He means "master", obviously,' explained Zeke. 'I've restored most of his functions but there's still a glitch in his speech pattern software. "As bad as I will be" means "as good as I was." He now pretty much says the opposite of what he means. But do not worry, you soon get used to it.'

'And you want me to go looking for water on a strange planet with *him*?' cried Kip.

'Please don't concern yourself,' Zeke assured him. 'He functions perfectly apart from what he says. You just need to do the opposite of whatever he advises you.'

Kip looked at him. 'An example?' he asked.

'Well, for instance if he tells you to stand still, you run. If he tells you to stand up, you sit down. Easy, really. Once we get back to our proper base, we'll work on that last little detail. We'll have him as good as new, won't we, Twerpy?'

'No, mistress,' said T-Twerpio. 'It's going to be terrible.'

Kip frowned. He wasn't sure about this at all but, at the same time, he couldn't afford to delay the rescue mission. Even though his visit here was running in real time, he'd have to be sure he could get to Mr Lazarus before the film credits began to roll. He could choose to leave the film now as Beth was advising him, but getting in and out was always risky and there was no guarantee he'd ever see Mr L onscreen again – after all, he was hardly a main character. If he stayed, Zeke would take him to Mr L. So for the moment, he would just have to make the best of things.

'Er . . . how are you?' he asked T-Twerpio.

'I am ill,' said the android. 'Damn you for asking.'

'Er . . . right,' muttered Kip. 'So that means . . . you're well and . . . thank you for asking!' He smiled, encouraged. He decided to try another question. 'So how . . . how did it feel being blown to bits?'

'It was wonderful,' said T-Twerpio. 'I would recommend it to everybody. I hope it happens to you some time.'

'See,' said Zeke. 'You are already conversing easily.' The spaceship started to judder as it moved into the planetoid's atmosphere. 'I would advise you to take a seat, my robotic friend,' he told T-Twerpio. He indicated the vacant one next to Kip. 'As soon as we're coming in to land, run a search for the nearest water supply, will you?'

'Get lost,' said T-Twerpio. Sitting down as instructed, he opened a hatch in his chest and started clicking buttons. Coloured lights pulsed and rippled on a display in there.

'Is it going to be hard finding water?' asked Kip politely.

'Yes,' said T–Twerpio. 'Slice of fish.'

'Eh?' asked Kip.

'I think that was "piece of cake,"' said Zeke. 'Like I said, it's usually the complete opposite but some things don't compute as easily.' The ship's fuselage began to shudder alarmingly. 'OK, my comrades,' said Zeke. 'Brace yourselves, we're going down.'

Kip settled back in his seat and held his breath as the *Trillenium Hawk* began its descent.

★ ★ ★

'Where are they going now?' asked Rose impatiently.

'They're landing on a small planet,' said Beth. 'Once they've repaired the spaceship, they'll be able to go after Mr Lazarus and his brother.'

Onscreen, they could see the *Trillenium Hawk* descending into what looked like a desert landscape. Powerful winds were blowing and the ship was swaying from side to side as it came down, its retro rockets blasting up great clouds of dust. Finally it settled into position and a bay door slid open. Bright lights clicked on and they could see Kip standing at the entrance with T–Twerpio beside him. The camera cut briefly to Kip's point of view. He was looking out across a windswept plain, devoid of trees or other vegetation. On a mountainous horizon, a couple of suns were setting in a blaze of blood red. It would soon be dark.

'I'm not sure I like the look of this place,' murmured Beth. 'You'd better be careful out there.' Kip didn't answer – he probably couldn't without being overheard, but he gave a kind of sigh that might have been some kind of agreement.

'Kip should tell them to get their own water,' said Rose darkly. 'There's bound to be something horrible waiting for him out there. There always *is* in this kind of film.'

But, as they watched, Kip and the metal creature began to descend the ramp and they set off into the gathering darkness.

★ ★ ★

Mr Lazarus lifted his head at the sound of approaching footsteps. He noticed that Dario had fallen asleep beside him and he jabbed an elbow into his brother's podgy side to wake him up. Dario grunted and said something terse, then blinked a couple of times and sat up straighter.

'Wassamarra?' he muttered.

Mr Lazarus nodded through the bars of the cell. A couple of Draconians were striding towards them. The first was one of the creatures that had brought the brothers down here in the first place, and Mr Lazarus noticed that he was now carrying some kind of weapon, what looked like a laser rifle, which was cradled across his chest. The other one, however, was clearly of a higher rank. He wore a purple cloak, a breastplate and a shiny black metal helmet. Around his scaly neck was a chunky metal device with a pulsing blue light at its centre. He stepped up to the bars and looked at the two brothers for a moment with his huge, yellow eyes, the pupils of which were vertical black lines. A forked tongue flickered in and out of his mouth.

Mr Lazarus was just wondering if he should say something when the Draconian saved him the trouble and spoke in a weird, unintelligible hiss that put Mr Lazarus in mind of fingernails scraping down a blackboard. He and Dario exchanged puzzled glances and then Mr Lazarus said, 'I'm sorry, I haven't the faintest idea what you're saying.'

The Draconian blinked and then nodded, as though he understood. He reached up a hand to the device around his neck and made a few quick adjustments. The blue light turned quickly to red, to green and finally to orange. The creature spoke again, and though the voice was still a skin-crawling hiss, now Mr Lazarus could understand what was being said.

'Ah, so you are human!' said the Draconian. 'I should have known from your repulsive appearance.'

'Look who's talking,' muttered Dario. 'You ain't exactly Johnny Depp yourself. I've seen better looking things on a fish counter. Why I—' He broke off with a gasp as Mr Lazarus jabbed him in the side again, but the Draconian didn't seem to have noticed the remarks. 'I am Commander Skelp,' he said. 'And this' – he gestured around him – 'is my starfighter.'

'Er...delighted to meet you,' said Mr Lazarus, trying to sound jovial. 'And what a magnificent spacecraft.' He got up from the bench and approached the bars, offering his hand to shake but the other lizard-man made a threatening gesture with the rifle, so he took a step back. 'I am Mr Lazarus,' he said. He gestured to the slumped figure on the bench behind him. 'And that, I'm afraid, is my brother, Dario. We're both very pleased to make your acquaintance.'

Skelp looked far from impressed. 'I'd like to know by what authority you have invaded my starfighter,' he croaked. 'And what was your intention in coming here at all?'

'Er . . .' Mr Lazarus grimaced. 'No intention at all, really. It was a bit of an accident, if you want to know the truth.'

Skelp's eyes widened in surprise. 'An accident?' he cried. 'Are you joking with me?'

'I would never do that,' said Mr Lazarus. 'You see, it's all my brother's fault. He'd had one or two drinks and he came to the place where I was working . . . the Paramount Picture Palace; I doubt you know it, a delightful little cinema just outside of Manchester and—'

'Silence!' snarled Skelp. 'Do you think I'm an idiot?'

'That's very hard to say,' said Dario, and Mr Lazarus winced. 'Having just met you for the first time. We can only hope you're smarter than you look.'

Skelp swivelled his head in Dario's direction, a look of disgust on his lizard-like features. He motioned to the creature beside him. 'Shoot the fat one,' he said, pointing at Dario, and the Draconian lifted his weapon to follow the order.

'Ah . . . no!' said Mr Lazarus, lifting his hands and taking another step forward. 'There's no need for that. You must forgive my brother, he's . . . er . . . he's an imbecile.'

Dario glared at him but clearly didn't want to risk saying anything else just now.

'Yes,' continued Mr Lazarus. 'Our mother dropped him on his head when he was little. Now he can't seem to help himself. All kinds of nonsense comes out of his mouth.' He lowered his voice a little and leaned closer to the bars, as though to confide a secret. 'Of course it wasn't an accident, us coming here,' he said. 'And I was a fool for even thinking you might fall for it.' His brain was racing as he tried to think of something that might get them out of trouble. The problem was that, although he'd screened several *Space Blasters* movies over the past few years, he only had a very sketchy idea of what actually happened in them. 'We . . . came here to warn you, Commander,' he said.

'Warn me?' Skelp's eyes narrowed suspiciously. 'About what?'

'Umm . . . about . . . a great danger that is

threatening to overcome you and your fellow…'
He struggled to remember the collective name for
the lizard-men. '…your fellow Delphiniums.'

'Delphiniums?' cried Skelp. 'Do you mean,
Draconians?'

'Isn't that what I said?' muttered Mr Lazarus. He
waved a hand at the translator around Skelp's neck.
'That thing must be defective.'

Skelp fiddled with the device. 'It sounded
distinctly like Delphiniums,' he muttered. 'Try it
again,' he hissed.

'Draconians,' said Mr Lazarus.

Skelp smiled. 'That's better,' he observed. 'Now
you're coming through loud and clear.' He stepped
closer to the bars. 'So…you were saying something
about a warning?'

'Er…yes. The er…rebel leader. What's his
name? Mike Starblaster.'

'Who?'

'Mark Skyjumper…er, Nick Stargazer…er, oh
you know, him with the teeth and the blonde hair.'

'Do you mean Zeke Stardancer?'

'That's the fellow! Yes, him. It has come to my
attention that he's planning a surprise attack on your
people.'

'I seriously doubt it,' smirked Skelp. 'Since my pilot has just blown his ship to smithereens.'

Mr Lazarus frowned. If that had actually happened then things had gone terribly wrong. He was certain the film's plot wouldn't allow its hero to be killed off in such a way. 'I wouldn't be so sure,' he said.

'No?'

'No. Those rebel types can be very sneaky. It might have been some kind of trick.'

Skelp frowned. He seemed to be thinking about it. 'Now you mention it, the *Trillenium Hawk* was seen to veer away in flames, but nobody actually saw it explode.'

'There you are then,' said Mr Lazarus. 'Now, my brother and I have vital information about a huge rebel offensive, set to take place in just a few days time. Our employers, the er...the *Friends of the Federation*, sent us here to warn you about it.'

'Yes,' agreed Dario, trying to back his brother up. 'We had explicit orders to get to you as quickly as possible.'

Skelp seemed unconvinced by this information. 'But I'm told that the two of you were fighting when you materialised.'

'Er, yes...' admitted Mr Lazarus. 'We er...' He glanced helplessly at Dario, looking for help.

'We're brothers,' said Dario, darkly, as though this explained everything.

'Exactly,' said Mr Lazarus. He turned back to Skelp. 'You know brothers,' he said. 'Don't you?'

Skelp nodded. 'My brother tried to turn my people against me,' he said thoughtfully.

'Ah, so you understand the problem. How did you deal with it?'

'I ate him,' said Skelp.

Mr Lazarus tried not to wince. 'An... unusual approach. But no doubt, very effective.'

'Did you have him cooked?' asked Dario. 'Or did you just eat him raw? And did you eat all of him or just a few choice parts?'

'I grow tired of this conversation,' Skelp warned them. 'Tell me what you know.'

'I'm afraid we can't,' said Mr Lazarus, with what he hoped sounded like genuine regret. 'The people who sent me here insisted that I tell nobody but the boss himself.'

'The boss?'

'Yes, you know who I mean, the Number One.'

'The big cheese,' said Dario. 'The head honcho.'

'The one who always keeps his face hidden under his cloak,' added Mr Lazarus.

'The emperor?'

'Yes, him. The Emperor Barkan . . . Larkan . . . ?'

'The Emperor Zarkan?'

'Yes, that's the one! Our words are for his ears only.'

'Hmm. And what if I decide to torture you both until you tell me everything you know?'

Mr Lazarus swallowed nervously. 'I'd really rather you didn't do that,' he said. 'I'm not very good with torture.'

'Me neither,' said Dario quickly. 'In fact, when I'm tortured, I just lie about everything. You really wouldn't be able to trust anything I told you. Not one word.'

Skelp smiled coldly. 'I have torture specialists on this ship, who could remove your skin and keep you alive for three whole days. In the end, you'd be begging for death.' There was a long, horrible silence while Skelp considered the situation. Then he shrugged his shoulders. 'But as it happens, we are on our way to visit the emperor, even as we speak. I wanted to tell him about our glorious victory over Stardancer. Now you seem to be suggesting that there *was* no victory. So you will have your opportunity to speak to the emperor. If he is not impressed by what you have to say, he'll probably throw you into the arena to fight for your lives against one of his pet beasts.'

'That's *something* to look forward to then,' said Dario drily.

Skelp regarded him for a moment and then gave Mr Lazarus a sly look. 'It only takes one of you to pass on the message,' he observed. 'If you like, I could arrange for your brother there to meet with an unfortunate accident on the way.'

Mr Lazarus glanced at Dario, who was still slumped on the bench, a glum look on his face. 'A tempting proposition,' he admitted. 'But I'd rather we both attended the meeting, if it's all the same to you.'

Skelp shrugged his shoulders. 'Your choice,' he said. He gestured to the other Draconian and the two of them turned and walked away.

'Could we have a little food in here?' Dario shouted after them. 'Maybe a glass of wine? A few nibbles?' But his requests were ignored. He looked at his brother. 'What was all that about?' he asked.

'It was about buying us a little more time,' said Mr Lazarus, returning to the bench. He sat down beside his brother. 'And, Dario, do me a favour, will you? The next time you decide to open your big mouth, please make sure you've got your brain in gear before you speak.'

'Huh,' said Dario. '*Somebody's* in a bad mood.'

CHAPTER ELEVEN

Tarka Daal

Kip and T–Twerpio made their way across the arid landscape of Tarka Daal. A chill wind blew low over the dry red earth, flinging flurries of stinging dust into their faces. Kip was horribly aware that time was ticking away and he was still no closer to finding Mr Lazarus. He glanced at the shambling, gawky figure of T–Twerpio beside him. The android had a large transparent canister strapped to his back, in which he was supposed to carry the water that Zeke needed. There was also a large reel of plastic hose. Kip couldn't help feeling it had been a mistake to agree to accompany T–Twerpio. He reminded himself that the answers to any questions he might ask had to be re-interpreted as they occurred.

'Do you know where we're going?'

'No.' (Which meant, yes.)

'Is it very far to the water?'

'A long way.' (Which meant, not far.)

'And . . . is it safe here?'

'Absolutely.' (Which meant, definitely not.)

Kip sighed, but somehow wasn't surprised.

'What's with the tin man?' asked a voice in Kip's ear and he was startled to be reminded that Beth was following all this in sound and vision. 'Time's moving on and he's just talking nonsense.'

'Didn't you see that bit?' whispered Kip. 'His software's on the blink.'

'Well, he needs to stop, because people are laughing.'

'What people?' hissed Kip.

'The audience.'

Kip's heart sank. He'd forgotten that his adventures (or at least, edited highlights of them) were currently being beamed to a cinema full of punters. What must they be thinking right now? *That kid looks like the guy who sold me some popcorn twenty minutes ago!* He remembered that several of his school friends were in the audience. And what if Dad decided to step into the auditorium for a look at the film? It didn't bear thinking about.

He decided to try T-Twerpio with a few more questions. 'Are there any dangerous life-forms on this planet?'

'Oh, no, none whatsoever.'

'I see.' Kip's stomach was starting to churn. 'And . . . the life-forms that aren't on this planet . . . would they be very big or very small creatures?'

'Tiny.'

'And . . . what would be our chances if they came after us?'

'Very high.'

This was beginning to sound like seriously bad news. The two of them were now climbing up a steep incline. On the skyline, the two suns had almost slipped beneath the mountainous horizon. 'Have you ever visited this planet before?' asked Kip.

'Yes, many times,' said T-Twerpio.

'So you're . . . pretty sure that you can look after us?'

'Slice of fish.'

'This is not sounding good,' hissed Kip for Beth's benefit.

'It's sounding downright dodgy,' whispered Beth's voice in his ear. 'Why don't you just go back to the spaceship?'

'Even if I do that, we can't *go* anywhere!'

They crested the hill and Kip had to snatch in a breath because they were looking down onto a huge lake of rippling water. The reflections from the dying light of the suns made it resemble a massive pool of blood.

'Wow!' said Beth's voice in Kip's ear, and then more faintly, he heard Rose say, 'That's fantastic!' He had to agree with them. It looked absolutely stunning.

'Let's stay right here and get the earth,' suggested T-Twerpio, and he led the way downhill to the shores of the lake. Kip followed, more cautiously, his gaze moving from left to right above the calm surface but, as far as he could tell, the area was deserted. T-Twerpio detached the end of the hose from the reel and dropped it into the shallows of the lake. He pressed a button on his belt and there was a humming sound as the hose was activated. The plastic container on the android's back began to fill with liquid.

Kip relaxed a little. This should only take a short while and then they would be on their way back to the security of the *Trillenium Hawk*. He scanned the horizon again. Still no sign of any other life form.

Then T-Twerpio said, 'Nothing's right.'

Kip glanced at him inquiringly. 'What do you mean, nothing's right? That means . . . something's wrong, yes?'

'No,' agreed T-Twerpio.

'Well, what is it?' asked Kip nervously.

'There's nothing going,' said T-Twerpio. Which meant that something *was* coming.

'Kip,' said Beth's voice in his ear. 'I don't want to worry you, but the music's gone all creepy... like something bad is going to happen.'

Music? He couldn't hear any music...

Kip remembered that the audience would be watching this with a soundtrack.

He tried to remain calm. He inspected the water tank, which was now about a third full. 'How do you know that... that nothing is going?' he asked T-Twerpio.

'Because my sensors aren't picking anything up,' said the android calmly. He opened the flap on his chest to reveal the rows of coloured lights within. On a small rectangular screen, something was flashing red. Kip looked wildly around, but still he couldn't see anything amiss.

'The music's getting louder!' Beth's voice warned him.

'Great.' He thought for a moment. 'Where's this nothing not going from?' he asked T-Twerpio.

'Above us,' said T-Twerpio, and despite himself, Kip looked up towards the sky, before realisation dawned on him and he returned his gaze to the lake. Now he became aware of a commotion below the surface, out towards the centre. As he looked, terrified, the disturbance intensified, the water bubbling and frothing as something huge came looming up from the blood-red depths. Suddenly, a great domed shape burst through the surface and at the same moment Beth screamed, nearly deafening him.

Kip had an impression of a big, scaly head from which a pair of baleful amber eyes glared across the churning water towards him. The head reared upwards, upwards, on the end of an impossibly long serpentine neck. It twisted left and right and then came back to rest its gaze upon the two vulnerable figures standing at the edge of the lake. A massive pair of jaws hinged open, discharging a long green tongue, which trailed saliva, and then the creature gave a shattering screech that seemed to turn Kip's blood to ice in his veins. He looked desperately at T-Twerpio, who was still calmly filling the backpack with water.

'What should we do?' he whispered.

T-Twerpio turned his metal face to look blankly at his companion. 'We must panic,' he said. 'And make as much noise as possible.'

Kip evaluated this comment as quickly as he could and translated it as, 'Stay calm and keep quiet.'

'But . . . that thing is looking straight at us,' he hissed. 'What if it's hungry?'

T-Twerpio turned his head to gaze across the lake. 'It's a beast of the earth,' he said. 'As long as we stay in the water, it can reach us. I suggest we stay right here, within reach of its short neck.' With that, he began to back away from the waterline. He pressed a button on his hip, which began smoothly letting out the length of hose as he went, keeping him connected to the water supply. Kip fell into step with T-Twerpio and the two of them moved slowly backwards up the incline, until they were standing a good distance from the lake. The tank continued to fill with liquid. It was now nearly two thirds full.

'We should be in danger here,' said T-Twerpio, happily. 'Slice of fish!'

Kip still didn't feel he could trust anything the android said.

The creature stayed where it was for the moment, its long neck craning high above the lake, its body still immersed. It seemed to be considering whether the two insubstantial creatures on the shore were worth pursuing.

'Kip, what are you doing?' whispered Beth. 'Why aren't you running away?'

'It's a water creature,' murmured Kip. 'T-Twerpio thinks we should be safe on dry land.'

No sooner had he said this, than the beast rose a little higher in the water and two long, scaly appendages thrust up from beneath the surface and spread themselves out like huge leather umbrellas.

'Oh great!' said Kip. 'Wings.' He looked at T-Twerpio. 'Now what do we do?' he asked.

'Stand absolutely still,' advised T-Twerpio, and turning, he began to run up the hill as fast as his spindly legs would carry him, unreeling the length of hose behind him as he went.

'Wait for me!' yelled Kip. He turned to run after the android but slipped on something under his feet. He went down on his backside and saw that he'd managed to stand on what looked like a turquoise jellyfish. He shook the thing off his foot, then looked up and saw T-Twerpio already disappearing over the brow of the hill; then he heard a great stirring noise behind him, the sound of air being displaced by something impossibly big, something that was launching itself up out of the lake.

Somehow, he couldn't stop himself from turning his head to look. His jaw dropped.

The lake creature was much bigger than he could have imagined, its body a long, serpentine twist of rippling muscle from which the two mighty wings extended, beating at the air and raining down torrents of water as it lifted itself clear of the lake and soared upwards, silhouetted against the dying suns. It was an image that might have earned its cinematographer an Oscar under different circumstances, but here in the twisted world of the Lazarus Enigma, it was one hundred per cent real and Kip was now in imminent danger of being swallowed whole.

'KIP, RUUUUUUUNNNNNNNNNNN!' Beth's voice nearly shattered his eardrums, galvanising him into movement. He came up into a crouch and launched himself forward, heading up the incline like an Olympic sprinter on steroids. As he neared the top of the hill, he was horribly aware of a great dark shadow enveloping him, a huge weight descending through the empty air onto his puny body. At the last moment, he flung himself over the crest of the rise and went down on his face, ploughing up dirt, the impact slamming the breath out of his body. The beast swooped over him and he was only dimly aware of two sets of talons, clicking shut mere inches above his prostrate body.

Then the creature was moving past across the plain, gliding higher on its outstretched wings. Kip saw that it was now homing in on the shambling, lurching figure of T-Twerpio, who was struggling along with the nearly full water tank on his back, seemingly unaware that disaster was closing in on him. The android looked so pathetic that Kip was moved to try and help him.

He stumbled upright and went in pursuit, yelling the android's name, trying to warn him to watch his back but, as he closed the distance between himself and his quarry, he saw the great flapping beast descend a second time, almost to the ground, some distance behind T-Twerpio. Its long neck whipped down and the jaws closed around something. Then the beast lifted itself skywards again and Kip saw that a long silvery line was dangling from the creature's mouth, trailing back down to the earth. For an instant, he didn't understand; then he realised that it was the hosepipe, the far end of which was still connected to the tank on T-Twerpio's back.

Kip quickened his pace, closing the last few yards between him and the android, yelling as he did so, telling T–Twerpio to disconnect the hose. But he didn't seem to be aware of anything but the need to escape. The hose was being pulled rapidly upwards like a long silver worm and very soon it would come to the end of its tether.

Kip was perhaps a couple of metres behind T–Twerpio when the hose was finally pulled taut and the android was lifted clear of the ground, kicking and struggling to no avail.

'Hurray!' Kip heard him shout and, without even thinking about it, acting purely on instinct, he raced across the distance between them and lunged forward, flinging himself headlong at the android's legs. His hands closed around T–Twerpio's ankles and suddenly he too was rocketing upwards at an alarming speed.

'Kip, what are you doing?' asked Beth, in his ear, but this wasn't the time to answer a question like that and it was too late to even consider why he had done such a foolish thing. Gritting his teeth against the rush of the air, he swung himself upwards, clawing his way higher up the android's back.

'Goodbye,' said T–Twerpio calmly. 'I fully expected to see you here!'

Kip ignored him, pulling himself higher still until

he could lift a hand to reach the water tank on T-Twerpio's back. He saw the place where the hose entered the tank and spotted a button labelled 'hose release.' Without considering the implications of his actions, he jabbed his thumb against the button. It was only in that same moment that he glanced down and saw how high they actually were.

And then the hose popped out of the socket with a dull *thunk* and suddenly, shockingly, they were falling back to earth.

CHAPTER TWELVE

Zarkan

Beth covered her eyes. She couldn't watch. On the screen, Kip and T–Twerpio were falling through the empty air. Then she heard Rose gasp beside her. 'What's happened?' she cried, pulling her hands away. She stared in disbelief at the screen. The image had changed. Now the camera had cut away to another scene entirely – a long shot of an eerie, high towered palace perched high on the side of a mountain. Beth knew this location from earlier films. It was the palace of the evil Emperor Zarkan.

'What are we doing *here*?' protested Rose. 'We need to know what's happened to Kip!'

'Kip!' Beth cried. There was no response.

Beth realised there was nothing they could do. Films ran in their pre-determined sequence no matter how affected they were by the arrival of characters who were not in the original script. 'I expect the director's trying to build suspense,' she said. 'He'll probably go back to Kip in a minute or two – film time isn't the same as real time.'

'Well, that's no use,' said Rose, huffily. She glowered at the screen. 'Who's that?' she pointed. Now the camera had cut once more to the interior of the palace, a long, veranda-style room, one side of which was a series of open stone arches that looked out onto a mountainous landscape. A strange tubby little creature was pacing restlessly up and down across the tiled floor, his arms behind his back. He was dressed in a uniform, a red frockcoat with gold epaulettes and white military-style trousers tucked into shiny black riding boots. His body was undoubtedly human but his head was that of an insect – a round shiny green blob from which two compound eyes stared unnervingly. A couple of purple antennae jutted out from the top of his skull.

'That's Jambo Jinks,' said Beth. 'He's Emperor Zarkan's personal assistant.'

'Urgh! He's a minger!' said Rose.

As if on cue, a second figure came gliding into shot – a tall, skinny man dressed in a drab cloak, the hood of which was up to hide his face. When he spoke, there was only a glimpse of his pale, gaunt features in the shadows.

'This had better be good, Jinks,' he said, in the hoarse, whispering voice he always used in the series. 'I was meditating.'

Jinks bowed obsequiously. 'A thousand apologies, Your Majesty, but I have just received news of the utmost importance and I thought you would want to hear it.' Jinks's voice by contrast was high and rather nasal.

Zarkan waved a hand impatiently. 'Speak then,' he suggested.

'Your Excellency, our forces have just received a message from Commander Skelp of Draconian Assault Force Five. A short while ago they came across and destroyed a rebel starship...'

'That's why you chose to interrupt my cogitations?' shrieked Zarkan. 'To give me news of no importance?'

'Your Stupendousness, please hear me out! This was no ordinary starfighter, but indeed a quarry you have been hunting for some considerable time. I speak of none other than the *Trillenium Hawk*!'

Zarkan stood there looking at Jinks in silence for several moments. 'You ... you're sure of this?'

'Absolutely, Your ... Your Wonderfulness. The Draconian pilot blasted it up the rear end with a laser cannon and it was seen to veer away, leaking smoke.'

There was another long silence. 'And . . . the pilot saw it explode?'

'Umm . . . I'm not sure that he exactly saw that, Your Fabulousness. He saw smoke and . . .'

'And what? What exactly did the pilot say?'

'That the . . . the ship veered away . . .'

'Leaking smoke, yes, yes, you said. But that could have been a ruse, obviously! It wouldn't be the first time Stardancer has used such a ploy, would it?'

'Er . . . I suppose not, your . . .'

'Where is Commander Skelp now?'

Jinks bowed again. 'He's on his way here, Your . . . Grace. He's bringing two prisoners with him, two earthlings who, it seems, are bringing news that is for Your ears only.'

Beth flinched as she realised that this must be Mr Lazarus and Dario. What were they planning? This would surely complicate things even more.

Zarkan shrugged his shoulders. 'So that's my day ruined then,' he observed.

'I beg your pardon, Your Eminence?'

'I said, that's my day gone down the tubes. There I was, thinking I might just spend this one chilling

133

with a bottle of Yalkin ale, watching a few reruns of *Best Gladiatorial Bouts Ever*, but no! No, Commander Skelp is dropping round. And you know how particular *he* is.'

'I . . . I . . .'

'Which means I'll have to have the palace tidied, get fresh flowers in, arrange for a decent dinner. Now, what can we give him? Not the Ilesian eel curry again, we've done that one to death. Marinated Grullbeast, perhaps, with a side order of spivelweed? No, we can't do that either, we served that to the Draconian envoy only last week!' He shook his head under the hood. 'Being an evil overlord is all very well, but people don't appreciate that it's a twenty-four hour job. I mean, when do I get any time for *me*?'

'Your Majesty, if I can be of assistance in any way. . .'

'Oh, you've already done your bit, Jinks. I mean, when Skelp said he was coming over, did it occur to you to check with me, see if I had anything planned?'

'Er, well no, I thought you . . .'

'"No, just come on over!"' Zarkan paced around a bit, clearly worried. 'What's Skelp's ETA?' he asked.

'Umm. He didn't say, Your Exemplitude.'

'Oh, he didn't say!' He mimicked Jinks's nasal tone. '"No worries, just pop in whenever you're ready; my master hasn't got much on today!" Oh, well that's marvellous, isn't it?' He reached into the pocket of his cloak and pulled out an electronic gadget. 'Well, we're just going to have to assume that he could be here at any moment.' He started thumbing a tiny keyboard on the device. 'I'm messaging everyone,' he said. 'I'll need to brief the team ASAP! Cooks, florists, cleaners, the works. Oh, and my personal stylist, of course.' He turned to leave, but Jinks halted him with a query.

'Er... your Splendidness? What of the Princess Shanna?'

'What *of* her?' muttered Zarkan.

'I was just... on my way down to see her. Do you have any instructions for me?'

Zarkan made a dismissive gesture. 'Just keep her under lock and key and make sure she's fed and watered. Her only importance to me is as a hostage, should Stardancer ever manage to find his way here. Now leave me alone and only contact me when you have a firm idea of when Skelp's spacecraft will be landing.'

'Your . . . Magnificence.' Jinks bowed as low as his tubby figure would allow and stayed in that position until the emperor had actually left the room. Then he straightened up with a sigh and made his way through a stone arch and down the long flight of steps that led to the prisons.

★ ★ ★

'Now where's he going?' asked Rose.

'To see Princess Shanna,' Beth told her.

'There's a princess?' Rose began to take more notice. She liked princesses.

Sure enough, now the camera had cut to a prison cell where an attractive young woman was sitting alone and forlorn on a rough stone bench. She wore a long green gown and her dark hair was braided into an elaborate arrangement. Despite being in such a dark and miserable place, her make-up looked immaculate. She lifted her head at the sound of footsteps, but seemed to sag when she saw who it was. 'Oh, it's you,' she said, with a strong American accent.

'You were expecting somebody else, Princess?' asked Jinks. He seemed amused.

'You know very well who I was expecting,' she told him haughtily. 'Zeke will be here before long and when he is, you and that bogus emperor of yours are gonna be real sorry.'

Jinks shook his head and his antennae wobbled. 'I'm afraid Mr Stardancer won't be coming,' he said calmly. 'You see, Princess, I have just received word that the *Trillenium Hawk* has been destroyed.'

'Destroyed?' Princess Shanna was moved enough to get up off her seat and walk closer to the bars. 'I don't believe ya,' she snapped. 'It's just another one of your lies.'

'Not so, Princess, though I confess it gives me no pleasure to tell you such news.' He too moved closer to the bars. 'If only you could cast your gaze further afield than some rough starfighter pilot and see that there are others in the world who admire you. Others who could offer you so much.'

Princess Shanna looked at Jinks and her expression turned to one of revulsion. 'You mean . . . are you telling me that . . . you mean *you*?'

Jinks reached out to clutch at the bars with his little hands. 'I know my appearance must be very unsettling to you, Princess, but I'm a man of means. I have a delightful villa here on Volpin Eight and I pull down a decent salary. With Stardancer gone, there are many here who will want to see you made an example of. I . . . I could be your ally . . . perhaps much more. I had hoped that perhaps you might feel a little something for me?'

'*Ewwww!*' Princess Shanna looked like she might be about to throw up. 'You think I want to go around with a half-man half-cockroach?'

Jinks looked at her in dismay. 'That's a bit harsh,' he said. 'I prefer the term insectoid, myself.' He looked past her into the cell and noticed a plate of untouched food on the floor beside the bench. 'Princess, you haven't eaten your lunch,' he chided her. 'I insisted that our cooks prepare you something you might like. I thought perhaps a traditional Earth delicacy . . .'

Princess Shanna shook her head. 'I'm not from Earth,' she told him. 'And I can't eat pastry, it goes straight to my hips.' She studied Jinks for a moment. 'Look, I don't want to seem rude, Mr Jinks . . .'

'Call me Jambo, please!'

'But . . . there's no way your people could have destroyed the Hawk. Zeke doesn't get caught unawares. It was probably just a trick to make you *think* he's out of the picture.'

Jinks sighed. 'That's what the Emperor said,' he admitted. 'But is it really so unlikely? After all, he's just a farm boy by birth. It's not as if he's a superhero or anything.'

Princess Shanna leaned closer to the bars. 'That's all you know,' she said triumphantly. 'Zeke can channel his inner cloak now. That's enough to give him the edge over you crummy Federation followers every time.' She extended a hand and showed Jinks a flashy-looking ring on her third finger. 'See this? Zeke gave me this before he left on his last mission. He told me that he'd come back to claim the ring and when he did, he'd ask me to be his wife.'

Jinks rolled his compound eyes. 'A ring,' he said, dismissively. 'Is that it? I can give you rings galore! Precious jewels, gold, exotic fragrances, you name it.'

'You don't get it, do ya?' said Princess Shanna, turning away and flouncing back to her bench. 'Me and Zeke, we're a team . . . and nothin's ever going to get in the way of that.' She sat on the bench and fluttered her eyelashes. 'Nothin',' she said, and the camera closed in on her determined expression.

Then, quite suddenly, the camera cut back to where it had left off – to Kip and T-Twerpio, tumbling head over heels to destruction.

CHAPTER THIRTEEN

Dinner Is Served

This wasn't looking good, Kip told himself. He clung on to T-Twerpio's twisting, rattling figure as they plummeted towards the ground. He could hear Beth screaming in his ear but in all the panic, he couldn't make out what she was saying.

'I think we're going to live,' he heard T-Twerpio mutter and could only agree with him. As they twisted to one side, he saw the *Trillenium Hawk* parked on a stretch of flat ground some distance away and he thought he caught a glimpse of a white-suited figure standing in the illuminated doorway, but then he spun round again and saw instead the hard, red earth rushing up to meet him at incredible speed...

He shut his eyes and braced himself for the impact. But it never came. Quite suddenly, the downward movement stopped. He opened his eyes again and realised that he and T-Twerpio were now floating, as if on a cushion of air, a few inches above the ground. He looked incredulously at T-Twerpio.

'What's happened?' he cried.

'My mistress has doomed us,' said the android matter-of-factly. With that, the 'cushion' seemed to evaporate and they dropped the last few inches with a soft thud. Kip realised what had saved them. Zeke must have sent out his inner cloak to provide them with a virtual crash mat. It was incredible that something that couldn't actually be seen could be so powerful.

But Kip had no time to dwell on this, because there was a loud shriek from high above them and, glancing up, Kip saw the flying beast descending at speed, its great jaws open to snatch them. He let go of T-Twerpio and the two of them scrambled upright and began to run back towards the *Trillenium Hawk*. Kip looked hopefully towards the open doorway but it appeared to be empty now and he had no option but to grit his teeth and run as fast as his legs would carry him.

He heard Beth's voice in his ear again, calmer now and oddly reassuring. 'When I say the word, I want you to move to your right,' she said. He risked a glance over his shoulder and wished he hadn't, because now he had a grandstand view down the open gullet of the advancing creature and it wasn't a pretty sight at all. Beth's voice was still talking him through it. 'Keep going. Wait for it, wait for it ... NOW!'

He angled sharp right and felt an abrupt rush of air as the beast skimmed by him, its talons missing their target by millimetres. Kip saw the beast soar on ahead of him, then wheel round and head back for another attempt. Beyond that, Kip glimpsed movement at the hatch of the *Trillenium Hawk*. Zeke was back but Kip couldn't see what he was up to and now the flying beast was zooming back towards him, growing bigger in his vision, blotting out everything else.

'Kip, this time, go left when I tell you,' said Beth's voice.

'I don't know,' gasped Kip. 'It looks like ... it might be ... expecting that ...'

'Trust me, Kip. Keep going straight until I tell you.'

Kip did as she told him, though the muscles in his legs were burning and his heart was hammering in his chest. The beast was so close Kip could see its eyes in hideous detail, tiny snakelike orbs with bright red pupils. The beast's jaws hinged open again and Kip could see row after row of sharp, yellow teeth, fringing the entrance to a pulsing, purple gullet.

'Now, Kip, NOW!' Beth's voice was a desperate yell, but Kip was mesmerised, unable to respond to her command, and those ferocious teeth were closing on him . . .

And quite suddenly, the beast erupted in a blaze of orange flame. It twisted sideways, passing so close to Kip that the wind threw him to the ground and he felt the heat of the fire as the stricken creature swooped by. It moved on a short distance, then struck the ground at an angle, smashing one wing to smithereens. Its body slammed hard into the earth, flinging up dust and Kip could see that its hind-quarters were an inferno of blazing fire. It thrashed around on the ground for a few moments, its serpentine neck lashing in its death throes until, finally, it lay still as the fire consumed it.

Kip sat there, stunned, staring at the destruction in open-mouthed shock. T-Twerpio wandered over, glancing at the burning beast as though it were nothing more than a rock. 'What a shame he didn't get you,' he observed.

Zeke came strolling over, a huge bazooka-like

laser gun slung across one shoulder. He grinned his film-star grin.

'That was close,' he said. He extended a hand and helped Kip to his feet. 'Didn't like risking a shot with you so near to that thing, but what else could I do?' He patted the weapon on his shoulder. 'My laser bazooka is a trusty weapon. Tell me, did you succeed in your mission?'

'I'm afraid not, mistress,' said T–Twerpio, slowing to a halt. He indicated the nearly full container on his back. 'And damn you for hindering us.'

'No problem,' said Zeke. 'Myself and Blooey have completed the repairs on the system so we'll replenish her water tanks and we'll be on our way.' He looked at Kip. 'You OK, young adventurer?'

Kip opened his mouth to say something but found he couldn't make words. Now that he was out of danger, his body was shaking.

'Here now, calm yourself,' said Zeke. 'You need to channel your inner cloak. Let's board the starship and make you a nice hot cup of Venusian tea. Then we'll chase those Draconians and see if they don't lead us to your ally and my princess.' He slipped an arm round Kip's shoulders and led him towards the open hatch of the *Trillenium Hawk*.

Within minutes, they had blasted off and were on their way again, using the *Hawk*'s in-built navigation system to follow the route taken by the Draconian starfighter. It wasn't until they'd been flying for quite a while that it occurred to Kip that he hadn't heard a peep out of Beth since he'd narrowly avoided the jaws of the space beast. He wondered if she'd even seen how the sequence turned out and he decided to say something to reassure her. That was when he pushed a finger into his right ear and discovered that the communication device was no longer there.

★ ★ ★

Mr Lazarus was just dozing off when he was rudely awoken by a jab in the ribs from Dario. He opened his eyes and glared irritably at his brother, then realised that somebody was standing at the bars of the cage. He saw that one of the lizard-men had arrived, carrying a tray in his scaly hands. He bent forward and slid it under the bottom bar.

'At last,' said Dario. 'I thought I was going to starve to death.' He got up from the bench and went to collect the tray. 'What took you so long?' he asked the Draconian. 'Do you treat all your guests this way? I've a good mind to write a letter of complaint.'

The creature just grunted and shuffled away.

'Hey! We're going to need a toilet break soon!' Dario shouted after him. 'You understand me? You can't keep us locked up like this. What about our human rights?'

'I'd save your breath if I was you,' muttered Mr Lazarus. 'He's not wearing a translator.'

Dario returned and took a seat alongside Mr Lazarus, balancing the tray on their combined laps. 'Well, at least they took notice of my request,' he said. The tray held two plastic beakers of a purple liquid and two plates covered by metal lids. Dario lifted one of the beakers and sniffed at it. 'Blackcurrant juice?' he muttered.

'I doubt it,' said Mr Lazarus.

Dario lifted it to his mouth and took a large gulp. He shook his head. 'It's not blackcurrant,' he agreed. 'It has a kind of meaty flavour. But it's not so bad.'

'How's your head?' asked Mr Lazarus.

'Like a tiny man is punching my brain. But I'll feel better when I've got some decent grub inside me.

Now, let's see what they've given us.' He lifted the cover on one of the plates and stared in dismay at what lay beneath it. The round white plate was filled with a large mound of pulsing, squirming green grubs, each one about the size of a man's thumb. 'What in the name of St Mina is this?' cried Dario.

Mr Lazarus smiled. 'It's the food eaten by a race of talking lizards,' he said. 'You were expecting spaghetti Bolognese?'

Dario scowled and lifted the other lid. This contained scores of shiny black beetles, skittering frantically to and fro on the plate. A high rim around its edge prevented them from getting away. Dario muttered something and replaced the lid. 'That's disgusting,' he said. 'Couldn't they have made us some toast or something?'

Mr Lazarus laughed. 'I don't know much about those creatures, but I wouldn't say grilling bread is a high priority on their planet.'

'Well, I've got to eat *something*,' protested Dario. 'I'm starving.' He reached down to the first plate and picked up one of the grubs between a pudgy thumb and forefinger.

'Don't even think about it,' Mr Lazarus advised him. 'You'll make yourself ill.'

Dario gave him a scornful look. 'I have eaten cuisine from all over the world,' he said. 'You think I can't handle this?'

He lifted the wriggling thing to his mouth and popped it in. Then he bit down on it. He began to gag, but got control of the reflex and started to chew, an expression on his face that suggested he was experiencing a bad smell. He swallowed with difficulty and reached for another grub, then offered it to Mr Lazarus.

'No thanks,' said Mr Lazarus grimly.

'Suit yourself.' Dario lifted the second grub to his mouth and popped it in. A trickle of green liquid ran down his double chin. 'You had any thoughts about what we can do?'

'I already told you. We can only wait and hope. Meanwhile, we need to cook up a convincing story to tell to this emperor fellow they're taking us to.'

'Don't look at me,' said Dario. 'That was your idea.' He reached for another grub. 'You know, these things aren't so very bad. They taste a bit like chicken.'

'I'll take your word for it,' Mr Lazarus assured him. 'And I made up the story as a delaying tactic.

149

That Skelp character was going to have his man shoot you.'

'I've met people like him before,' said Dario.

Mr Lazarus raised his eyebrows. 'Really?'

'You know what I mean. All talk. He was never going to follow through with that.'

'Oh, so you're the big expert on lizard-men now, are you?' Mr Lazarus scowled. 'Maybe I should have let him shoot you.'

'Don't be like that,' said Dario. 'I'm your little brother. You're supposed to look after me.'

'It's funny,' said Mr Lazarus, 'but right now it's all I can do to keep my hands from going around your throat.'

Dario laughed at this. 'You've got to get a grip on yourself,' he said. 'I don't know if I ever told you this, but—oh!'

He broke off suddenly, a look of alarm on his face. His normally ruddy features had turned rather pale.

'What's the matter?' asked Mr Lazarus.

Dario put down the plate of grubs and placed a hand on his huge stomach. 'I don't feel so good,' he said.

'I told you not to eat these things.'

'Nobody likes a person who says "I told you so!"' observed Dario. 'It's just...' He stood up suddenly, upsetting the tray. The dishes clattered to the floor and black beetles went skittering in all directions. 'I think I'm going to be sick,' he said.

'Dario, don't do that. There's no window in here...' But it was no use. Before Mr Lazarus could stop him, Dario stumbled to the furthest corner of the small room and began loudly parting company with his strange dinner. Mr Lazarus shook his head as the room filled up with the distinctive aroma of partially digested grubs. He could only hope it wouldn't be too long before they reached their destination.

CHAPTER FOURTEEN

Worse

'Kip, can you hear me? Kip? Say something, you idiot!'

Beth was beginning to get annoyed. On-screen, she could see that Kip was back in the comparative safety of the *Trillenium Hawk*, chatting with Zeke and Blutacca as they went in pursuit of the Draconian starfighter, but he seemed unable to hear a word she was saying. Which meant that either his communicator had packed up or he had lost it, most likely back on that horrible planet. She looked down at Rose. 'It's no good,' she said. 'He can't hear me.'

'So what happens now?' asked Rose grumpily. 'Do we have to wait here while Kip flies through outer space? That could take *ages*.'

'It won't,' Beth assured her. 'The film is only two hours long, remember and it's already been running . . .' she glanced at her watch '. . . for thirty five minutes. Kip could actually be in there for two years, but all we'll see is edited highlights of what's happening to him. The running time is always the same.'

Rose looked thoughtful and then shook her head. 'I don't understand,' she said.

'It *is* hard to get,' she admitted. 'But, look, supposing you went to see *Sleeping Beauty*, OK?'

'I *love* that film,' said Rose.

'Good. Well, the princess is asleep for a hundred years, right? But obviously you couldn't sit there and watch it for a hundred years, could you? That would be boring. So the film-makers just show you key bits of what happens while she sleeps. The edited highlights. And that's what we're watching now. Bits of what Kip's up to. The most interesting bits.'

'What happens if he can't find Mr Lazarus?'

Beth frowned. 'Well, he has an escape device with him, the Retriever. As long as he presses the eject button before the film ends, he'll be fine . . . and as long as he's hanging on to Mr L—'

'And his brother?'

'Yes, as long as he's hanging on to them, they can all escape together. I just hope that Kip realises that if he can't get to Mr L, he should come out and save himself.'

'Save himself from what?' asked Rose.

Beth was about to attempt an answer when the door of the projection room burst open suddenly. Beth turned in dread, expecting to see Kip's dad standing there, demanding to know what was going on – but instead, she saw Stephanie Holder in the doorway with an outraged expression on her face. She still had the camera hanging around her neck.

'What do you want?' asked Beth nervously.

Stephanie strode into the room, the braces on her teeth flashing in the light of the projector. 'I'd like to know what the hell's going on here!' she said.

There was a long silence while Beth stood there, open-mouthed, trying to think of a suitable answer. In the end all she could come up with was, 'You're not supposed to be in here. This is for staff only.'

'Is that right?' Stephanie snorted, her hands on her hips. 'Well, tough! There's something very fishy going on.' She pointed to the viewing hatch. 'Perhaps you'd like to explain to me how it is that Kip McCall has got a role in the new *Space Blasters* movie? And the mysterious Mr Lazarus, for that matter.' She pointed towards the viewing hatch. 'I've been sitting out there mesmerised,' she said. 'At first, I couldn't believe it. I saw that Mr Lazarus and I said to myself, you must be mistaken, it's probably just an actor who *looks* like him. And then the next thing I knew, there was Kip. And there can't be two kids in the world that look like that!'

Beth stared at her. 'He...he...'

'He won a talent competition!' said Rose. 'In a movie magazine.'

'Er...yeah!' said Beth, shooting Rose a grateful smile. 'Yeah, that's right. The winner got to be in the new film. He...he won it ages ago, didn't he, Rose?'

'Yes. Months back.'

'And...and Mr Lazarus went along to look after him, you know, in Hollywood and everything and, well, I guess they must have offered him a part in the film too.'

Stephanie looked far from convinced. 'And how come this was never mentioned to me before? Like when I interviewed Kip about the launch?'

'Er...well, he...he wanted it to be a surprise,' explained Rose. 'He didn't tell *anyone*.'

'Apart from us, obviously,' added Beth.

'I see. So if I go down to the foyer and mention it to his father...'

'Don't do that!' cried Beth hastily.

Stephanie's eyes narrowed behind the frames of her thick glasses. 'Why not?' she murmured.

'Because ... he doesn't know about it, either,' said Beth. 'Mr McCall ... doesn't approve of that kind of thing. Kids being in films and all. He ... he'd only be cross if you told him.'

Stephanie gave a derisive laugh. 'What nonsense!' she cried. 'If Kip had won a part in the film, I think they'd have written him better dialogue than the twaddle he's been coming out with.' She gazed thoughtfully around the room. 'Where *is* he, anyway?'

'He ... went to get a choc-ice!' said Rose.

'Oh, so he'll be down in the foyer then? Good, I'll ask him about it.' Stephanie turned as if to leave the room but Beth bounded past her and closed the door, putting her back against it.

'He's not really in the foyer,' she admitted.

'I knew it,' said Stephanie. She turned and moved closer to the projector. 'He's in the film. And that Mr Lazarus is in there too ... and the other guy who sounds just like him. A relative, I shouldn't wonder. Am I right?' She turned to look back at Beth. 'Mr McCall said something about an invention that the old man had come up with. Something that made cinema seem more real...' Now her gaze fell on the apparatus beside the projector. 'What did he call it? The Lazarus ... something or other.'

'Enigma,' murmured Beth, and she couldn't help glancing at the apparatus as she did so.

Stephanie walked over to where Beth had looked. She reached out a hand and touched one of the metal bars that ran alongside it. Beth noticed that her fingernails were painted a dark shade of green with little gold sparkles on their tips. 'So this ... invention?' murmured Stephanie. 'It somehow projects an image of a person into a film? Makes it look as though they're interacting with the characters?'

'Er ... yeah,' said Beth, glimpsing a possible way out of this. 'That's exactly right. It's just a fake thing, really.'

'No, it's not,' said Rose defiantly, and Beth could have cheerfully strangled her. She looked proudly at Stephanie. 'It *really* puts you into the film. I know, I've been in one. I was chased by numbertails and everything.'

Stephanie looked down at her in disbelief. 'How could it?' she cried. 'Put you in the film, I mean. That's not actually possible...' She looked at Beth. 'Is it?' she added.

Beth sighed and realised the game was up. 'I'm afraid it is,' she said.

Stephanie looked down at the wooden platform. She seemed to be trying to figure something out. 'But that's ... barmy,' she said.

'I agree,' admitted Beth. 'But there you go.'

Stephanie turned and stared at her. 'So you're telling me that Kip McCall is ... *literally* in the film.'

Beth nodded. 'It's hard to get your head around,' she admitted. 'It makes more sense once you've been in there.'

'Are you saying that you've done it too?'

'Well, er ...'

'She was in *Terror Island* with me,' said Rose helpfully. 'And she was in *Spy Another Day* cos she fancied Daniel Crag!'

Stephanie stared at Rose for a moment, as though wondering whether or not to believe such a ridiculous tale. Then she shrugged. 'Well, one thing's for certain,' she said. 'I need to go down to the foyer and tell Kip's father what's going on. And then I'm going home to write the story.'

'You can't!' protested Beth. 'It has to be kept a secret.'

'Oh, really? And why's that?'

'Because... if it all came out... it could mean the end of the Paramount Picture Palace. Mr Lazarus would have to leave and... there'd be all kinds of trouble.'

'Can't help that,' said Stephanie. 'This is in the public interest. My readers have a right to know what's going on under their noses. I'm not saying they'll believe it, but... they do have the right. So if you'll just stand aside, I'll—'

'NO!' shrieked Rose; and without warning, she launched herself at Stephanie, arms outstretched. Her hands slammed into Stephanie's chest, knocking her off-balance. She staggered backwards a step and her wedge heels connected with the edge of the apparatus. Then she sat down hard, her skinny bottom thudding onto the wooden platform. Her own impetus did the rest. The platform slid smoothly forward on its oiled wheels and she went with it, trundling backwards into the light. She sat there for a moment, looking startled. She opened her mouth to say something. And then she was gone.

'Rose!' cried Beth. 'What have you done?'

Rose turned back from the Enigma, an innocent expression on her face. 'I was only trying to help,' she said, and Beth began to understand why Kip always complained that his sister got away with everything she did. The two of them stood there looking at each other for a moment. Then there was a loud grunt from onscreen and a gasp of surprise drifted up from the audience. Without another word, Beth and Rose ran to the viewing hatch to look at the screen. There was the scene just as it had been a moment before: Kip, Zeke and Blutacca in the gleaming interior of the spaceship. T-Twerpio was trundling to and fro in the background, apparently serving drinks. Only now there was a new addition. Stephanie Holder was sitting in Blutacca's lap and, as Beth and Rose watched, she looked up into the Silonian's hairy face and began to scream.

Kip stared at Stephanie in absolute disbelief. The journalist was pretty much the last person he had expected to see here. As he watched in stunned silence, she scrambled frantically out of the Silonian's lap and backed off several steps.

'Egret sneeple dumplethong?' muttered Blutacca, which probably meant something like, 'What's her problem?'

Stephanie stood there, looking around in a kind

of wide-eyed panic, as though trying to puzzle out where she was. Finally, her gaze fell on Kip. 'What . . . what's happened?' she gasped.

Kip wasn't sure what to tell her. He knew from experience that film characters hated hearing that they didn't really exist and there was no way he could say anything without Zeke and Blutacca overhearing him, so: 'You're on the *Trillenium Hawk*,' he said. 'Calm down, you're safe here.'

'Is this young lady with you?' asked Zeke.

'Er . . . yeah. Kind of,' admitted Kip. 'She's a . . . sort of a . . . I work with her.'

'She's with the Rebel Alliance?'

'Er . . . yeah, that's right.'

'And she's from Earth also?'

Kip nodded. He glared at Stephanie, warning her not to contradict him, but she was so deeply in shock she seemed unable to say anything at all. She just stood there with her mouth open like a stranded codfish.

Zeke turned to look at Stephanie and gave her his dazzling grin. 'Greetings, young lady, don't worry. Nobody's going to hurt you – and old Blooey there looks a lot fiercer than he really is.'

Stephanie stared at him. 'But you're . . . you're

Mike Hamble!' she observed, using the name of the actor who famously played Zeke in the *Space Blasters* films.

Zeke shook his head. 'I think you've confused me with somebody else,' he said. 'My name's Zeke. Zeke Stardancer.' He got up from his seat and moved towards her. 'Would you mind telling me how you got here?'

It was evident that for Stephanie, everything was moving much too fast. 'I . . . went up to the projection room, because I saw him . . .' she waved a hand at Kip '. . . in the film.'

'The film?' Zeke seemed puzzled by the term. 'What film?'

'Well, I was at the launch night of *Space Blasters*,' mumbled Stephanie. 'And I—'

'I think what she means,' interrupted Kip, 'is that she went to one of our, er . . . transporter rooms, because she . . . she had an urgent message for me. And she needed to deliver it in person, because we know how the Federation listen in to our audio messages.' He fell back on his geeky knowledge of the *Space Blasters* series. 'You know of the rebel coalition movement on Spandex Seven?'

'Er . . . yes,' said Zeke. 'I've heard of it.'

'And you know the transporter rooms the Federation used to move freight between galaxies? Our unit, the Firestorm Fighters of Innit Poo Val, captured those transporter rooms in a skirmish with the Federation. And now we use them to move our agents from place to place through the space-time continuum. That's right, isn't it, Stephanie?'

The reporter looked at Kip, confused. 'Is it?' she asked. 'I don't . . .'

'This happens a lot,' Kip told Zeke. 'Those freight transporters aren't really designed for use on actual living beings. It can make you a little mixed-up for a while. I tell you what, is there somewhere she can rest for a few minutes, while I have a quick chat with her?'

'Of course. I'll get Twerpy to take you to one of the guest cabins.' Zeke looked thoughtfully at the new arrival. 'Stephanie,' he murmured. 'What a lovely name.'

Now Stephanie looked even more astonished. 'You . . . you really think so?'

'Oh yes.' He stepped a little closer and lifted a hand to brush Stephanie's hair out of her eyes. 'Are there many like you on your planet?' he asked her. 'I'd heard that the Earth was famous for its beautiful women, but I had no idea . . .'

There was a long embarrassing silence and then T–Twerpio stepped forward, bowed politely and said, 'If you would hate to walk away from me, sir?'

Stephanie managed to tear her gaze away from Zeke's blue eyes for a moment. 'I . . . beg your pardon?' she said.

'Don't get him started,' Kip advised her. 'Come on. We need to talk.' He got up from his chair, grabbed Stephanie's arm and pulled her along behind T–Twerpio's gangling figure. They followed him out of the flight room and along a white painted corridor.

'What's going on?' hissed Stephanie.

'It's very simple,' Kip whispered back. 'You're now in the movie. Thing is, how did you get here?' This was getting way too complicated for his liking. As if things weren't bad enough, he now had a nosy reporter to contend with. How would he get everybody back to the projection room?

'I saw you in the film so I went up to the projection room. There were two girls in there. Beth and a younger one. She pushed me . . .'

'Rose,' murmured Kip. 'That's my little sister.'

'Little brat, more like! I said I was going down to

the foyer to tell your dad what was going on and she ran at me and pushed me onto this wooden thing . . .'

'The Enigma. Yes, it figures.'

T–Twerpio had stopped in front of a metal door. He pressed a button and it slid sideways to reveal a small, sparsely furnished room within. 'There we're not,' he said. 'I trust you'll be very uncomfortable. If there's nothing you require, don't press that red button.' He indicated a green button set into one of the walls. 'Hello,' he said and walked away.

'His voice circuits—' began Kip, but Stephanie waved him to silence.

'I've been watching the film,' she reminded him. 'I know what his problem is.' She looked around the room for a moment and then walked across to a sofa and sat down. She placed a hand on her left shoulder and reacted when she didn't find what she'd expected. 'Oh, no!' she gasped.

'What's the matter?' asked Kip.

'I had a camera,' she said. 'A really expensive one. Now it's gone.'

'You must have lost it on your way in,' Kip told her. 'It happens.'

'But . . . it's not even mine,' she protested. 'I

borrowed it for the launch. What am I going to tell the owner?'

Kip could only shrug. 'Maybe it'll turn up,' he told her, but he didn't think there was much chance of that. If it had been dropped on entry it had probably skipped off into some other part of the film. It had happened last time. Only then it wasn't a camera that was lost. It was Beth.

There was an uncomfortable silence. 'Why did you pretend that I was working with you?' asked Stephanie at last.

Kip came and sat beside her. 'It's hard to explain. See, that guy out there, that's not Mike Hamble . . . it really *is* Zeke Stardancer.'

'How can it be?' asked Stephanie. 'I mean, I understand that we're somehow in the film, but surely . . .' She seemed to remember something. 'Whatever he's calling himself, he's got the hots for me!' she said with a smile of satisfaction.

'Oh, I don't think so. No, he's in love with Princess Shanna. Everyone knows that. We're on our way to rescue her now.'

'I know the story. But didn't you see the way he was staring at me? He said I was *beautiful*.'

Kip looked at her doubtfully, taking in the unruly

hair and the massive metal-encrusted teeth. 'Maybe he was just being nice,' he said. Stephanie looked offended but he ignored that. The last thing he needed right now was another complication. 'Anyway, like I said, it's all real out there and what we can't do is go round mentioning films and stuff. They don't like it . . .'

'They?'

'That lot.' Kip waved a hand in the general direction of the *Hawk's* cockpit. 'The characters. They all believe they're real. Well, they *are* real. You know like in the film, T-Twerpio and Blooey would be played by actors, dressed up? Well, now there's nobody inside those costumes. In fact, they aren't even costumes. That's a genuine android and a genuine Silonian. We've got to . . . you know, play along? So if anybody asks, you work with me.'

'But how can such a thing be possible?' cried Stephanie.

'It's the Enigma. It's what it does. And listen, there's no point in asking how it works; even Mr Lazarus doesn't know that and he invented it.'

'But surely, it's dangerous here, isn't it? I saw a big monster on the screen before. It nearly ate you! How do we, you know, get back?'

167

'I've got a way of doing that,' Kip assured her. 'But we can't use it until we find Mr Lazarus and his brother. I'm worried that if I leave the movie now I'll never be able to find them. The four of us will have to make the trip back together.' He frowned. 'I hope it works,' he said. 'I've never tried it with more than three people at one time.' He considered for a moment. 'On second thoughts, maybe I should take you back now,' he said. 'Then try to come back and look for the others.'

'Oh, don't worry,' said Stephanie. 'I don't want to go back yet. This is just about the most amazing thing that's ever happened to me. It could be the scoop of my career. And, besides . . . I've always had a bit of a crush on Mike Hamble.'

'Zeke!' Kip reminded her. 'His name's Zeke.'

'Whatever,' said Stephanie.

'And . . . you have to understand, these movie characters, they act a certain way because that's what they're programmed to do in a film. I mean, Zeke is supposed to be in love with Princess Shanna, right? But she's not here now, so maybe he's just saying the kind of stuff to you that he's supposed to be saying to her. Do you see what I mean?'

But Stephanie wasn't listening to him. She was

staring around, wide-eyed, taking in every detail of the room. Kip understood. He'd been like this the first time he went into a movie. He sighed and got to his feet. 'Let's head back out there,' he suggested. 'Just act like you've done this kind of thing a hundred times before.'

Stephanie jumped up with apparent eagerness. She started towards the door and Kip followed her. 'I've always wanted to be in a movie,' she told him, as the door slid silently open and they stepped out into the corridor. 'But I never thought it would happen to me.' She grinned. 'It's fun, isn't it?'

'Oh yeah,' said Kip. 'It's always fun. Till things start to go wrong.'

'What could go wrong?' Stephanie asked him.

'Everything,' he said. 'Trust me, I've done this before.'

CHAPTER FIFTEEN

A Tangled Web

Mr Lazarus woke from another half-slumber as the room around him began to vibrate. He could hear a deep, booming sound coming from somewhere below him and he glanced at Dario, questioningly.

'I think maybe we're coming in to land some-where,' said Dario. He still looked pale and delicate after his bout of sickness. 'Let's pray they have a toilet I can use.'

Mr Lazarus grunted. 'I would say a toilet is the least of our worries,' he muttered. He had spent the hours before sleep had finally overtaken him planning out some kind of story that he might tell Emperor Zarkan. He was uncomfortably aware, from what he remembered of the earlier films, that the emperor had a habit of treating those who displeased him rather roughly.

The sound of approaching feet announced that they had visitors once again. He saw that Com-mander Skelp was approaching the cell, flanked by an escort of two armed Draconians. He stopped a short distance away and gestured to one of the men. The Draconian placed his hand against a lit panel on the wall and the metal bars slid silently aside.

'We have arrived on Volpin Eight,' he announced, as though this should mean something to them. 'I've come to escort you to the emperor's palace.'

'Never mind about that,' said Dario getting to his feet. 'You can start by escorting us to a loo. My bladder is bursting.'

'A ... *loo*?' Skelp seemed unfamiliar with the word. 'What does this word mean?'

'A toilet,' explained Mr Lazarus. 'A lavatory? We've been cooped up in this cell for ages. We need to ... you know ...'

'Ah.' Realisation seemed to dawn on Skelp's lizard-like features and he nodded. Then his nostrils twitched as he caught an unpleasant aroma. 'What's that smell?' he demanded.

'My brother has been sick,' Mr Lazarus told him. 'I'm afraid your Draconian food disagreed with him.'

Skelp's face registered disapproval. 'Disgusting,' he muttered. 'You humans really do have some vile habits.'

'At least we don't eat our relatives,' muttered Dario under his breath.

Skelp gestured impatiently at them. 'Move yourselves,' he told the two captives. 'We will pause at a toilet on our way out, but don't go getting any ideas about escaping. My men are just itching for a chance to use their weapons. One blast from their laser rifles and your bodies will melt into a pool of quivering fat.'

'Not so very different in my brother's case,' observed Mr Lazarus.

'Watch it!' snapped Dario, irritably.

'We have no intention of trying to escape,' Mr Lazarus assured Skelp. 'We came to deliver a message to the emperor, remember?'

'It had better be good,' Skelp warned him. 'The Emperor Zarkan is not one to suffer fools gladly. You'd do well to remember that.' He motioned them forward. 'Well, come along, we haven't got all day.' The two captives stepped out of the cell and the Draconian troops arranged themselves on either side of them, then led them briskly along the white-painted corridor.

'Who's your decorator?' asked Dario. 'Only this looks a bit minimal for my liking. You might consider a nice floral wallpaper . . . maybe some drapes.'

'Silence!' snapped Skelp irritably. 'You really are a most annoying creature.'

They walked a short distance and then came to a halt at a metal door. 'The er...facilities,' announced Skelp. 'We'll wait here for you. Don't be long, the emperor doesn't like to be kept waiting.'

He waved a hand at a sensor and the metal door slid smoothly aside. Mr Lazarus and Dario hurried in and the door closed behind them. They stood for a moment, looking around at what appeared to be a perfectly ordinary washroom, a series of cubicles on one side of it, a row of washbasins along the other. It was evident at a glance that there was no other way out of here. Dario hurried straight to a cubicle and went inside, closing the door behind him. Mr Lazarus thought for a moment, then followed his brother and rapped gently on the door with his knuckles.

'What are you doing?' he hissed.

'What do you *think* I'm doing!' came the irritated reply. 'I'm writing a symphony.'

'There's no need to be sarcastic. OK, listen to me. I've been putting the finishing touches to our story. We will tell Emperor Zarkan that we have uncovered a plot to assassinate him.'

'Huh? That's the best you could come up with?'

'Well at least it's *something*. Do you have a better idea?'

'We could say we'd been sent to read the gas meters. Then we could warn them there was going to be an explosion and, in the panic, we'd make our escape.' There was a long pause. 'On the other hand, maybe your idea is better,' he admitted. 'I don't even know if they have gas meters in space. But what do you hope to achieve?'

'Well, I'm hoping that the emperor will believe us and want to know more details. We'll give him some line about how we still don't know the full story, but we have ways of finding out. Hopefully, it will make him hesitate about having us put to death.'

There was a long silence. 'That could happen?' asked Dario nervously.

'Judging by what I remember from the earlier films, yes. He's not the nicest person you could ever wish to meet.'

There was the sound of a toilet flushing and then the door opened. Dario looked even paler than before. 'Why did you bring me into this crazy film?' he cried. 'Why couldn't you have chosen something gentle? Something *funny*?'

Mr Lazarus could hardly believe what he was hearing. 'With respect, Dario, it wasn't really my choice that we ended up here. I seem to remember...' He broke off as Dario barged past him to the line of washbasins on the opposite wall.

'I'm not listening to you,' Dario informed him. 'As usual on these occasions, you're just using this as an excuse to get at me.' He pressed the handle of a tap and what looked like green syrup spurted into the bowl. 'Oh no, what's this?' he cried. 'They don't even use water. These people are like animals!'

'They *are* animals,' Mr Lazarus reminded him. 'Lizards. And as I understand it, lizards are not the most compassionate of creatures. So for once in your life, Dario, listen to your brother. Whatever I say when we meet this emperor fellow, just agree with me, OK? Back me up.'

Dario was sluicing the green juice over his hands. He leaned forward and sniffed at them. 'Actually, this stuff doesn't smell too bad,' he observed. 'Kind of a citrus aroma.' He seemed to think for a moment. 'This emperor... what's he emperor of, exactly? A planet?'

'If I remember correctly,' said Mr Lazarus. 'He's Emperor of the Universe.'

Dario gave a low whistle. 'The entire Universe? That's pretty important, huh? So . . . he must be a very rich man, yes?'

'Dario . . .' began Mr Lazarus.

'No, I'm only saying, I bet he's got a bit of wealth tucked away somewhere. Diamonds, maybe? Gold? Other precious metals?'

Mr Lazarus sighed. This was beginning to sound familiar. He turned away and headed to the cubicles. 'We're doomed,' he said. He went into a cubicle and shut the door behind him.

★ ★ ★

Back in the cockpit of the *Trillenium Hawk*, Zeke and Blutacca were still at the controls. When Kip and Stephanie entered, Zeke directed his dazzling smile in her direction.

'Ah, Stephanie,' he said. 'Feeling better?'

She nodded. 'Much better, thanks. I'm sorry if I seemed a little . . . confused back there.'

'Do not concern yourself,' said Zeke. 'It must be exhausting travelling that way.' Once again, he was looking at her as if she were some kind of goddess. Kip didn't get it. He knew that looks weren't everything but she wasn't a patch on Princess Shanna, but then, as Kip had tried to explain to Stephanie, Zeke was programmed to fall for a woman in this movie – maybe with no Princess Shanna in sight, he had fixed his aim on the first female who happened along.

'You know,' continued Zeke, 'if you'd like a guided tour of the Hawk, you only have—'

'Where are we heading?' interrupted Kip, impatiently.

'Hmm? Oh.' Zeke managed to tear his gaze away from Stephanie for a moment. 'Er . . . we're following the same route the Draconian starfighter took. It looks as though they're headed for Volpin Eight.'

Kip's sharp intake of breath must have alerted Stephanie to the fact that this wasn't good news.

'What's Volpin Eight?' she asked, panic all over her face.

'It's Emperor Zarkan's home planet,' Kip told her. 'People usually just call it Death World.' He hoped Mr Lazarus and Dario were OK.

Stephanie frowned. 'That sounds like a theme park you wouldn't want to visit,' she observed.

'Oh, don't be afraid, fair one,' said Zeke. 'I will never let you out of my sight.'

Stephanie simpered. 'Really?' she asked. 'Promise?'

'By my honour and my Gredi oath,' said Zeke.

'Never mind all that nonsense,' said Kip sternly. 'You need to keep your mind on the job. Volpin Eight, eh?'

'Yes, who'd have thought that the Emperor would be there?'

Kip looked at Zeke in disbelief. Plotting was never the strong point in these films but it wouldn't have taken Sherlock Holmes to work out that Zarkan would probably be based on his home planet, and that, wherever he was, Princess Shanna was likely to be also. A four-year-old kid could have worked that out. 'You've never visited the planet before, have you?' he said.

Zeke's blue eyes narrowed. 'How do you know that?' he asked. 'I am puzzled, Kip, you seem to know an awful lot about me. How has this come about?'

'I know *everything* about you,' said Kip. 'Every little thing. I know you were born on the planet Trelfarb. I know that, after the death of your parents, you were raised by your Uncle Neville and your Aunt Sally. I know that you have a star-shaped birthmark on your chest . . .'

'Really?' said Stephanie, looking suddenly very interested.

'Yes, would you care to see it?' asked Zeke.

'No, she wouldn't!' snapped Kip. 'I know it all, Zeke. Before I came on this... this mission, I did a crash course on you. So I know that you've always steered clear of Volpin Eight before, because you couldn't figure out a way to get past the planet's defence system. Everyone in the Alliance has rated it as a suicide mission.'

'I cannot deny it,' admitted Zeke. 'But Blooey and I have come up with a cunning plan.'

'Stredgonk nadda!' agreed Blutacca, nodding his hairy head.

'You see,' continued Zeke, 'I now have something I didn't have before... something the Emperor doesn't know about.'

'The ability to cloak!' said Kip.

'Exactly. Our plan is to get just outside the range of the planet's warning systems. Then I'll cloak the entire ship and we'll go in undetected. We'll land a short distance from the palace and we'll approach it on foot. And then...'

'Then?' prompted Kip.

'Well, we haven't actually settled on a plan for

that bit,' admitted Zeke. 'But it sounds ingenious up to there, don't you think?'

Kip considered it. 'You really believe you're powerful enough to cloak the entire *Trillenium Hawk?*' he asked.

'Of course he is!' said Stephanie indignantly – though Kip could tell that she didn't really have any idea what she was talking about. She took the opportunity to move closer to Zeke and placed a manicured hand on one of his broad shoulders. 'Zeke's strong enough to do anything.'

Kip felt like asking her what she knew about it, but decided against it. 'OK,' he said. 'So we go in there and...'

'And we rescue your friends,' said Zeke matter-of-factly. 'Then we get out of there. Mission accomplished.'

'And Princess Shanna?' Kip reminded him.

'Who?' Zeke looked puzzled.

'Princess Shanna,' said Kip slowly. 'Your true love? The woman you're supposed to be marrying?'

Stephanie took her hand off Zeke's shoulder as though it had suddenly become too hot to touch. 'You're engaged?' she shrieked.

'Er . . . not officially,' said Zeke, hastily. 'Of course, we're good friends, but . . .'

'You gave her a ring,' Kip reminded him. 'You told her the next time you saw her, you'd make her your wife.'

'Your knowledge of my past is unnerving,' said Zeke. 'You did not witness this, did you, young traveller?'

'I know *everything*,' Kip told him. 'And that's what you said to her. "Shanna, the next time I see you, I shall make you my wife." It's famous.'

'Umm . . . well, whatever I said, of course we'll have to rescue the princess.'

'What's she like, this Princess Shazza?' asked Stephanie with a scowl.

'It's Shanna,' Kip corrected her.

Zeke shrugged his brawny shoulders. 'Oh, she's . . . nothing special,' he said.

'She's beautiful!' cried Kip, thinking of the poster in his bedroom. 'She's a cracker! She's the best-looking girl in the Universe.'

'Well, I would advise you not to believe everything you read in those polls,' Zeke countered. 'And remember, the planet Earth was not included.' He gave Stephanie a meaningful look. 'Recent

181

experience tells me the women of Earth are particularly beautiful. I think that's why they weren't included. Too much of an unfair advantage.'

'Do you really think so?' Stephanie started to simper again and Kip felt like throwing up.

'We have got to keep on track here,' he warned Zeke. 'You made a promise to Princess Shanna in the last . . . the last . . . recently and you can't go back on it. She's counting on you.'

'Relax,' Zeke told him. 'It's not as if I'm going to abandon her, is it? No, I'll get her out of there. That's what I promised I'd do at the last Alliance meeting. But she has to understand . . . a man's liable to change his mind. Not everything is set in stone.'

'No,' agreed Stephanie. 'Quite right, Zeke. A man's . . . gotta do . . . what a man's gotta do.'

Kip glared at her, wishing she'd stay out of this.

'Grundle thampa dipthong Volpin glip,' announced Blutacca and everybody turned to look at him. 'Snedgle flange lump bongo natwee.'

Zeke translated for them. 'Blooey says that according to his monitors, the Draconian starfighter is touching down on Volpin Eight, right about now. If we continue at our current speed, we'll only be an hour or so behind them.'

Kip told himself that this would be an hour or so in real time, which would hopefully be compressed to just a few minutes in the film's running time. He was horribly aware that the minutes were ticking away and he seemed to be no closer to reaching his objective. What's more, he had no way of knowing how long the movie itself had been running back at the Paramount. At this stage, he could only hope that he'd find Mr Lazarus before it was too late.

CHAPTER SIXTEEN

Volpin Eight

Mr Lazarus and Dario stood at the entrance of the Draconian starfighter and watched apprehensively as the craft's huge hatch hinged forward and down, revealing the scene outside.

'Mama mia,' said Dario and Mr Lazarus had to agree. Ahead of them, in the weird greenish light of day, they could see a huge white marble courtyard, and gathered upon it there must have been thousands of Draconians – men, women and children – presumably assembled to witness the arrival of the starfighter and its human captives. A narrow walkway led through the midst of them, a short distance to the entrance of a huge palace, constructed from gleaming white stone. Its ramparts rose to giddy heights and these were topped by even taller spires that reared up, it seemed, almost to the clouds. The entrance to the palace was guarded by row after row of heavily armed space troopers.

'Behold the palace of his magnificence, the Emperor Zarkan, undisputed ruler of the Universe,' said Commander Skelp, who was standing beside the brothers. He gave them a stern look. 'A few words of advice,' he muttered. 'You do not speak in the emperor's presence unless given express permission to do so. You keep your heads bowed at all times and you do not question anything he tells you. Do I make myself clear?'

'Perfectly,' said Mr Lazarus.

'Sure, whatever,' said Dario.

'Come then.' Skelp led the way down the ramp and the brothers followed, flanked by their ever-watchful armed guards. As they stepped from the ramp onto the stone courtyard, the huge crowd seemed to erupt into a frenzy of cheering and arm waving. Some of them were holding flags and banners written in an unidentified language.

'They seem very happy to see us,' said Dario cheerfully.

'Of course they are,' said Skelp. 'Humans are a great delicacy on Volpin Eight.'

'A . . . delicacy?' croaked Dario. 'You don't mean . . . ?'

'I'm afraid he does,' said Mr Lazarus, and Dario gulped loudly.

'That's disgusting,' he said.

Skelp glanced over his shoulder and allowed himself a sardonic smile. 'Let's hope the information you hold is important enough to save your necks,' he said. 'The emperor generally puts on a feast when I visit – and I must confess, I'm partial to a few rashers of human myself.'

The brothers exchanged worried looks, but there was nothing to be said right now. They followed Skelp through the roaring, braying crowd. Occasionally, a scaly hand reached out to prod at them, as if testing the plumpness of the meat. Perhaps not surprisingly, Dario received more prods than his skinny brother.

'Do you mind?' he snapped, when one woman gave him too hard a pinch. 'That's very rude!'

'Take it easy,' Mr Lazarus warned him, but he couldn't help noticing that the woman who had done the prodding, a plump creature dressed in a silk gown and a strange, feathered hat, was actually salivating as she reached out.

Mr Lazarus swallowed nervously. He considered the lie he had constructed and wondered if it would be enough to save them from what seemed like a rather grisly fate. He sighed, thinking to himself that he wouldn't have to wait long to find out.

★ ★ ★

Back in the projection room, Beth and Rose were doing their best to follow what was becoming an increasingly weird storyline. Furthermore, they could sense that the audience was getting more and more restless out there. Each new revelation was met with murmurs of disbelief and it was surely only a matter of time before somebody decided to walk out. Beth wasn't sure what would happen then. Meanwhile, Kip seemed no nearer to finding Mr Lazarus and Beth was unable to contact him.

'I think Kip needs some help,' said Rose. 'I think he's enjoying being in the film too much and he's got carried away. Maybe one of us should go in there and see if we can sort things out.'

Beth looked down at her in dismay. 'Don't even think about it,' she said. 'Things are complicated enough.'

'Yes, but . . .'

'No buts! I'm not even sure Kip's done the right

thing going in there himself. What if he can't get out?'

'Could that happen?'

'Yes,' said Beth miserably. 'I'm afraid it could.'

'So I'd have a brother who I could only ever see if I watched this film?' Rose gestured to the clattering projector alongside them.

'Yes, that's pretty much what would happen.' She looked at Rose. 'But . . . I'm sure it won't come to that,' she added.

Rose considered for a moment. 'There must be some way we can talk to him.'

Beth shook her head. 'There isn't, not without the . . .' She broke off as a memory came back to her. A memory of when she and Kip had just arrived on the beach of Terror Island, looking for Rose, and Kip's mobile phone had started ringing. The caller had been Kip's dad, checking that everything was all right. The situation had required some pretty frantic improvisation.

Beth reached into her pocket and pulled out her mobile. Rose looked at it scornfully. 'That won't work . . . will it?'

'It just might.'

'But they're in outer space,' reasoned Rose.

'No they're not. They're only *there*.' Beth pointed to the projector, the length of film rattling through the gate. 'It worked once before. Anyway, it's got to be worth a try.' She switched on the phone and pressed the memory button. There was Kip's number, stored in prime position. She glanced through the hatch and made sure Kip was still off screen. The last thing she wanted was to cause another blooper, with Kip talking on a mobile in a spaceship. She saw that Mr Lazarus and Dario were climbing the steps to the palace, so this seemed as good a time as any. She offered up a little prayer and pressed 'call'.

★ ★ ★

When the phone in Kip's pocket started shrilling, he nearly fell out of his seat in surprise, but he had to admit, it was a welcome interruption. For what felt like hours, he'd been sitting in the cockpit listening to Zeke and Stephanie bill and coo at each other like a pair of characters from a Jennifer Aniston movie. Zeke seemed to have forgotten all about Princess Shanna. Just before the phone rang, he'd been telling Stephanie all about his home planet of Trelfarb and wondering if she wouldn't like to visit it sometime. Kip pulled the mobile from his pocket and saw Beth's name on the display. He lifted it to his ear and tried to make his voice sound as normal as possible.

'Oh, hi,' he said. 'How're you?'

'Better now that I can talk to you. What happened to your communicator?'

'Think I must have lost it on Tarka Daal,' he said. 'I'd forgotten about the phone thing.'

'Me too. Rose reminded me. Are you OK?'

'Yes. Can you er . . . see me on screen?'

'No. Right now I'm looking at Mr L and his brother. They've arrived on this planet . . .'

'Er . . . oh yeah, that'll be Volpin Eight.'

'OK. Well, there's like thousands of those lizard-men things and they all look very hungry, they keep poking Dario like they can't wait to eat him.'

'Nice.'

'And they're going into this big building, with all these space troopers standing around it.'

'That'll be the Emperor's palace,' said Kip. 'Well, we should be there in an hour or so.'

'An hour or so? Kip, you haven't got that long, the film's been running . . . nearly fifty minutes now.'

'Yeah, but you know how this works. It'll edit me as it goes along. Don't worry, it's all good.' Kip was aware that both Zeke and Stephanie were studying him intently. 'It's er . . . it's kind of difficult to talk right now,' he said. 'But it's good to know I can ring you if I need you.'

'Kip, I don't know what to do. The audience is getting really restless.'

'The . . . audience?'

'Yes. I wouldn't be surprised if they start walking out soon. And I keep thinking your dad's going to come in and see you up on the screen and if that happens, what am I supposed to tell him?'

Kip cringed. He felt completely helpless. 'What can I do?' he asked her. 'I've got to stay in here until I can get to Mr L— Er, I mean, Barty Skythump!''

'Barty who?'

'Never mind!'

'The thing is, Kip . . . if it looks like you're getting to the end of the film and you still haven't found Mr Lazarus . . . you *will* do the right thing, won't you? You will press the eject button?'

'Course I will.'

'You promise?'

'Look, I'd better go now. Things to do.'

'Kip, promise me!'

'Catch you later!' Kip hung up on her and went to slip the phone back into his pocket, but Zeke held out a hand for it.

'Show,' he said.

Kip sheepishly handed him the phone and Zeke studied it, turning the device around in his hand. 'What is this?' he asked. 'You have a fondness for vintage items?'

'That's state-of-the-art, that is,' Kip told him. 'I got it for Christmas.'

'Christ-Mass?' Zeke seemed unfamiliar with the word. 'Who were you talking to?'

'Oh, just my... my contact in the Alliance. Yeah, she was telling me that the Draconian ship has landed and Barty and his brother, they're being taken to see Emperor Zarkan.'

Zeke's mouth twisted into a grimace of distaste. 'Let's hope we get to him before it's too late,' he said. 'The emperor is not known for his generosity of spirit.'

'It sounds like you don't care very much for him,' said Stephanie, who clearly wasn't that familiar with the *Space Blasters* storyline.

'I hate him,' said Zeke and, for once, his grin had

deserted him.

'But why, what did he ever . . . ?'

'Because of what happened to my father.'

'Ah,' said Stephanie uncomfortably. 'What was it, some kind of neighbourly dispute? I know those things can get out of hand. When was this, exactly?'

'I was just a child. I was away when Zarkan and his space troopers called. He left my father lying in the dust. I found him on my return.'

'He was . . . sunbathing, was he?'

'No, Stephanie, he was dead. Murdered at Zarkan's order.'

'Oh, I see. That is rather . . . unfortunate. Can I ask why he . . . ?'

'Because of the prophesy, of course. The Prophecy of Chingarl.'

'The . . . ?'

Stephanie was clearly mystified so Kip tried to help her out. 'The Chingarl prophesy was in the first . . . It was when Zeke was very young. It was found written on a cave wall and it said that a blond-haired child, born on the planet Trelfarb, would one day become Emperor of the Universe. Zarkan heard about it, so he sent his men to kill all the male children on the planet under the age of eight. But Zeke was visiting his uncle and aunt on Larkspur, so he was spared.'

'That's like something out of the Bible,' observed Stephanie.

Probably where the screenwriter got the idea in the first place, thought Kip but he didn't say anything.

'My father tried to stop the massacre and paid with his life,' said Zeke. 'My mother was a broken woman after that. She never really recovered. She died just a few months later and I went back to live with my aunt and uncle. I've spent my life telling myself that one day my parents' deaths will be avenged,' growled Zeke. 'Maybe that time is almost at hand.'

'Oh, I don't know,' said Stephanie, taking his hands in hers. 'That's a big commitment. I think you should perhaps send the emperor a very terse letter, telling him how you feel and threatening him with legal action if he doesn't buck his ideas up.'

Zeke looked at her incredulously. 'He killed my father,' he reminded her. 'Murdered him in cold blood.'

'Yes, and I'm not saying that's right. But . . . well, could you perhaps place the matter in the hands of the police or . . . whoever handles that kind of thing in outer space?'

'No, Stephanie.' Zeke shook his head. 'Your words are wise and I value your advice . . . but this is something that's been coming for a long time now. A man can only run away for so long. Then one day, he has to stand and fight.'

'Yes, but you see, that's exactly when things can get out of hand. I knew a chap back in . . . on Earth, who decided he didn't like a garden shed that his neighbour put up, so he decided to take matters into his own hands and . . .'

'Stephanie,' said Kip. He shook his head. 'I don't think it's really the same thing, is it?'

She thought about it for a moment. 'I suppose not,' she said.

'Meeble grumple snardle-prong,' said Blutacca, and they all lifted their gazes to look at him. 'Greep snong, tinkle flot, adjul thweet.'

Zeke nodded and looked at the others. 'Blooey says we are nearly in range of Zarkan's early warning sensors,' he said. 'The time has come for me to cloak the ship.' He gave Stephanie an apologetic smile. 'This is going to take a lot of concentration on my part, so I'm afraid we'll have to stop talking now. You can tell me all about this man and the garden shed later. Strap yourselves in,' he told them. 'Just in case we should happen to take a hit. The next time we speak, hopefully, we'll have set down on Volpin Eight.'

Stephanie leaned closer. 'A kiss for luck,' she said and planted a noisy smacker on Zeke's lips. Weirdly, he seemed pleased by this and his famous grin returned. He watched as Stephanie and Kip strapped themselves into their own seats. Then he settled back, closed his eyes and began to concentrate . . .

CHAPTER SEVENTEEN

Zarkan Returns

Mr Lazarus and Dario followed Commander Skelp through the entrance doors of the palace. Marble columns rose all around, supporting a ceiling, which seemed to stretch above them at an incredible height. They crossed a tiled hall and went in through another doorway where they found themselves in a large room, the walls of which were hung with massive paintings, each one featuring a hooded figure, the faces barely visible; Zarkan's ancestors, Mr Lazarus supposed. In the centre of the room stood a long trestle table, which was heaped with foods of all kinds, some of which actually looked edible.

Dario perked up when he saw the spread and started to move towards it, but was brought to a standstill by a terse command from Commander Skelp. 'Stay where you are!' he growled – though he looked very pleased with the welcome the emperor had laid on.

Dario looked at him defiantly. 'But we're starving,' he complained.

'Nonsense, you were fed on the way here, I made sure of that.'

'Yes, with lizard food,' said Dario. 'Bugs and beetles! It made me sick to my stomach.'

'Nevertheless, you will wait until the Emperor arrives. And even then you shall eat nothing unless he invites you to partake.'

Just at that moment, the space troopers ranged around the room snapped smartly to attention as two figures came in. The first was cloaked and hooded, like the figures in the paintings, and seemed to glide across the tiles like some kind of ghost. The second, a portly creature with the head of an insect and the uniformed body of a man, waddled along a short distance behind. The cloaked character drifted across to the table and one gnarled hand reached towards what looked like a large bunch of grapes.

'Hang on, greedy chops,' said Dario, before Mr Lazarus could stop him. 'We're supposed to wait till the emperor gets here.'

There was a long silence. The hooded face turned to inspect Dario and a pair of amber eyes seemed to glow with anger as they glared out from shadow.

'Who has the impudence to speak to me in such a fashion?' said the cloaked figure in a weird, sighing whisper of a voice. 'Commander Skelp, what is the meaning of this?'

'A thousand apologies, your Magnificence,' said the Commander, bowing his head. 'You must make allowances for them. These humans are very primitive creatures. They're really little more than dumb animals.'

'That's good, coming from you,' observed Dario, and Mr Lazarus glared at his brother in an attempt to silence him.

'These are the captives you spoke of?' hissed the emperor. 'These two...idiots?'

'Indeed, your Majesty,' said Skelp, bowing again. 'They materialised aboard my ship and immediately began to fight with each other.'

'How distasteful. I must say they are disgusting-looking specimens. It would surely be more of a mercy to put them out of their misery.'

'Who says we're miserable?' muttered Dario. 'I'm known for my cheerful disposition. Laughing Dario, that's what these used to call me back in Naples! I did stand-up comedy for a living. People laughed at me when I said I wanted to do it, but they soon stopped laughing when they saw me on stage.'

'Yes, that was the main problem,' muttered Mr Lazarus.

'Of course, I would have had them killed instantly,' continued Skelp, ignoring his captives, 'but they insisted that they had important news that was for your ears only.'

There was a long silence. Then the fingers of the wizened hand plucked a lush, green grape from the bunch and lifted it into the shadows of the hood. There was a loud, slobbering sound and some noisy chewing, which seemed to go on for ages. Only when he had finished eating did Zarkan speak again. 'You.' He pointed a grey finger at Mr Lazarus. 'You seem less of an imbecile than your companion. What have you to say for yourself?'

Mr Lazarus bowed respectfully. 'Your Majesty, I am Matteus Lazarus of the planet Earth. I have news of the greatest importance, something I feel sure you will want to know about. I didn't want to risk entrusting it to anybody else.'

The hooded head nodded almost imperceptibly. 'Go on,' said the emperor.

'It has come to my attention, Your Majesty, that there is a plot to assassinate you.'

Zarkan made a smirking sound. 'Is that all? I would think that at any given moment, there must be hundreds of creatures around this Universe with similar intentions. Apparently, I'm not very popular with some of them.'

The insect-headed creature beside the emperor made a strange chirruping noise, which Mr Lazarus eventually realised was laughter. 'Oh, Your Majesty, that's very funny!' Jinks said. 'Not popular! Very good.'

The hooded head turned in the creature's direction and he stopped laughing. 'You find me amusing, Jinks? You think I'm comical? Would you perhaps like me to perform a few cartwheels for your entertainment?'

'Er . . . oh, no, Your Incredibleness, not at all. I was merely commenting . . .'

'Well, don't. When I want your opinion, I'll tell you what it is.'

Jinks bowed his head humbly and Zarkan returned his attention to Mr Lazarus. 'Can you give me one reason why I shouldn't send you straight to the gladiatorial arena to be eaten by my pet Krylls?' he asked.

Mr Lazarus wondered what Krylls might be, but this was hardly the time to ponder the matter. 'Only, Your Majesty, that the person that has sworn to overthrow you is somebody I think you already know. A man by the name of, er... Zeke Stardancer.'

'That's impossible,' said Jinks, taking a step forward. 'Stardancer is dead. Commander Skelp himself reported that the man's starfighter had been blown to pieces, only a few hours ago.'

Skelp's lizard eyes flickered open and shut a few times. 'To be fair, I never said it was blown to pieces. Only that it was leaking smoke and looked to be out of control.'

Zarkan laughed derisively. 'What did I tell you, Jinks? Stardancer's no fool, he and I have been playing this little game too long for him to make such a silly mistake.'

'You... play games with each other?' muttered Dario. 'What, like Ludo... Monopoly?'

'The emperor was speaking metaphorically,' snapped Jinks.

'A man of Stardancer's abilities is not going to be eliminated as simply as that,' continued Zarkan. 'Obviously it was a trick.' He turned back to look at Mr Lazarus. 'So when and where is this assassination attempt to take place?' he asked.

'That's the problem,' said Mr Lazarus. 'I don't know... yet.'

'What kind of an answer is that?' cried Jinks. 'Stop speaking in riddles and give His Magnificence a straight reply to His question.'

'Well, I...'

'It's simply not good enough! Now stop beating about the bush and...' Jinks stopped talking as the emperor lifted a clenched fist and pointed it in his assistant's direction. Mr Lazarus saw that he had a chunky gold ring on his index finger – and in that instant, a bright purple light shot out of the ring and bathed Jinks in a shimmering glow. Instantly, he froze in his steps and stood there, as silent and immobile as a statue.

'What did you do to him?' asked Mr Lazarus.

'He was starting to get on my nerves,' said Zarkan. 'Now, go on with what you were saying. But don't take all day.'

'Umm... no, Your Majesty. I was trying to explain that I have to determine exactly when this event will take place. And, to do so, I need a little more time to listen in to the Rebel Alliance's transmissions.'

'Hmm. And how do you propose to do that? You don't appear to have any equipment with you.'

'Oh, I have everything I need, right here,' said Mr Lazarus, tapping the side of his head. 'I have established a psychic link with the Alliance's network. As soon as they announce their plans, I will know of them.'

'That's right,' said Dario. 'My brother is psychic. He's brilliant. He used to have a nightclub act. Why, I bet he could tell you what you're thinking, right now!'

Mr Lazarus shot a warning glare at his brother but it was too late. The amber eyes beneath the emperor's hood seemed to burn with fresh interest. 'A psychic, eh? Now that *is* interesting. Very well, tell me. What *am* I thinking?'

Mr Lazarus pondered for a moment. He couldn't afford to get this wrong. He'd have to go for something pretty obvious. 'You are thinking . . .'

'Yes?'

'You are thinking mostly two things: one, that I could be playing for time . . . and two, that my brother is a complete idiot.'

Zarkan cackled softly. 'Very impressive,' he said. 'That's exactly right. Well, perhaps we *shall* allow you a little more time. Let's say... twenty-four hours. And then if no information about this supposed assassination attempt is forthcoming, you and your stupid brother shall visit the arena tomorrow and be the first to face my Krylls. Till then, you shall be my guests...'

'Oh, that's very kind of you,' said Dario, moving towards the dining table.

'In the cells,' added Zarkan coldly.

'But surely, you won't mind if we take a little refreshment first,' pleaded Dario. 'We're absolutely starving. We haven't eaten anything decent for days now.'

'Step away from the table,' murmured Zarkan.

'You surely wouldn't begrudge us a little something?' Dario reached out a hand towards the bowl of grapes, but Zarkan was too quick for him. The clenched fist came up, a ray of purple light shot out from his signet ring and Dario froze, just as his fingers closed around a sprig of grapes. 'Take them down to the cells,' said the emperor, waving a hand at a couple of space troopers. 'They can keep our other prisoner amused for a while. Meanwhile, Commander Skelp, you are my honoured guest, please help yourself.'

Mr Lazarus watched as a couple of space troopers moved across to Dario and lifted him up in their arms. He was as stiff and unbending as a post. He still had some of the grapes clutched in his chubby fingers.

'What have you done to my brother?' asked Mr Lazarus anxiously. 'Is he dead?'

'Of course not,' sneered the emperor. 'The effect is temporary. A pity.' He cast a glance in Jinks's direction. 'Both of them are easier to tolerate when they're like that.'

The Troopers carried Dario towards an exit while a third man prodded Mr Lazarus in the back with the barrel of his gun and he was obliged to follow the others, out of the room and down a flight of stairs.

CHAPTER EIGHTEEN

Allies

A few minutes later, Mr Lazarus found himself being pushed in the direction of another cell. It looked much like the one he and Dario had occupied aboard the Draconian starfighter. The only difference was, this one was already occupied by a beautiful young woman, dressed in a long, flowing gown. Mr Lazarus thought he recognised her from the earlier movies. The stout metal bars slid aside and the woman watched in silence as Mr Lazarus was thrust into the room and then as Dario was carried in and propped in a corner like some incredibly lifelike statue. The three Draconians left the cell, and an instant later the bars slid silently across the entrance, sealing it. The Draconians muttered a few unintelligible grunts and headed back up the stairs to the ground floor.

Mr Lazarus smiled at the woman. 'If I remember correctly,' he said, 'you are the princess, are you not?'

'Princess Shanna,' she told him imperiously. 'You're supposed to go down on one knee when you address me, but in these circumstances I suppose we can overlook it.' She studied Dario for a moment. 'I see that the Emperor's been using his freezing ray again,' she said. 'That big bully.' Then her lovely dark eyes fastened on the sprig of grapes still clutched in Dario's fingers and she made an eager beeline for them. She pulled them from his grasp and crammed them into her own mouth. 'You must excuse me,' she said, her mouth full. 'Those Draconian beasts have given me nothing I can eat all day.'

Mr Lazarus gestured to the tray of food on the floor by the bench. 'And that?' he murmured.

'Pastry,' she said as though this explained everything.

'You can't eat pastry?'

'Not can't. *Won't*! I put on weight if I even *look* at the stuff.'

'In that case, I wonder if I might ... ?'

'Be my guest,' she told him. He went over to the bench, picked up the tray and sat down, placing it on his lap. He lifted the metal lid from the plate, half expecting to find the same disgusting meal he'd been offered on the starfighter, but found what looked like a perfectly serviceable meat pie, with mashed potatoes and green vegetables. He grabbed a fork and scooped up a mouthful of mash, crammed it into his mouth and swallowed it gratefully. It was stone cold, and the gravy a bit congealed, but it was like heaven to his empty stomach. 'You could have eaten the vegetables,' he suggested.

'With that gravy all over them?' Princess Shanna shook her head. 'It's not easy maintaining this figure. But grapes are zero points on the Celestial Diet.'

'I don't think I've heard of that one,' said Mr Lazarus, munching a mouthful of pie.

'Oh, everyone's doing it,' Princess Shanna assured him. 'Everyone who's *anyone*.' She nodded in Dario's direction. 'So what did your friend do wrong?' she asked.

'He's not my friend, he's my brother,' Mr Lazarus corrected her. 'And I'm not sure. He can be a bit . . . annoying sometimes. I have to admit Dario is easier to handle like that but I'm told the effect isn't permanent. I'm also wondering if I should save him a bit of pie.'

Princess Shanna waved a manicured hand in front of Dario's face and evoked no reaction whatsoever. 'It doesn't look like he's going to be in any condition to eat for some time,' she said. 'And judging by *his* figure, it wouldn't harm him to go without for a while.' She crammed the last grape into her mouth and studied Mr Lazarus thoughtfully. 'You seem to know who I am, but I don't know you.'

'Forgive me. I am Mr Lazarus, from . . . from the planet Earth. Nice to meet you. I understand you're a good friend of Nick Starjumper . . . er . . . Mike Skyrunner . . . er . . . Zeke Stardancer!'

The princess perked up at the mention of Zeke's name. 'You know him?'

'Well, only by reputation,' Mr Lazarus assured her.

'And do you have any idea where he is?'

'I'm afraid not. But I'm sure he'll be doing his very best to get here and rescue you. That's the . . . sort of chap he is.'

'Yeah,' said Princess Shanna fondly. 'That's him in a nutshell, isn't it?' She came over and sat beside Mr Lazarus, looking at the remaining food on his plate with a horrified expression. 'Why has the emperor taken you prisoner?' she asked.

'Because I sort of accidentally ended up on one of his starships.'

'Wow. Sort of accidentally? How did that happen?'

'It's . . . complicated,' said Mr Lazarus. 'Perhaps we should just leave it at that.'

'I hope Zeke gets here soon,' said Princess Shanna. 'Only it's very dull, being a captive. I've been stuck in here for ages.'

'I'm sure you'll be rescued before too long,' Mr Lazarus assured her. 'I'm kind of hoping to be rescued myself.'

'By Zeke?' cried the princess incredulously.

'No, by somebody else. Anybody else really, I'm not fussy.' He placed the last bit of food in his mouth and chewed thoughtfully. 'I must admit, I thought outer space would be a bit more interesting than this. Since I arrived, I've done nothing but sit around in cells, feeling bored.'

'Tell me about it,' said Princess Shanna. 'I must've been here for weeks. They won't even give me any exercise equipment.'

At that moment, a low groan issued from Dario's lips and his stiff body became suddenly pliant. His legs buckled under him and he slipped down the wall onto his backside. He sat there, blinking around the room in confusion.

'Wh ... what happened?' he muttered.

'Oh, Dario, you're back,' observed Mr Lazarus. 'I'm afraid we're still prisoners.' He was horribly aware of the tray on his lap, containing an incriminating, gravy-stained plate. Dario's gaze fell on it immediately and hope glimmered in his eyes. 'They gave us food?' he croaked.

'Oh, this?' said Mr Lazarus. 'Well, you were out cold and we didn't know when you were going to come back to your senses, so ...'

'So what?' growled Dario.

'I ... I ate it.'

'You didn't save anything for me?' Dario looked suddenly outraged. He stumbled to his feet. 'Your own brother? Not even a taste? That's terrible! If it had been the other way around, I would have saved the entire meal for you. I wouldn't have even tasted it.'

'Oh, well then, the outcome would have been the same,' said Mr Lazarus. 'So that's good.' He set the tray down on the floor and indicated Princess Shanna. 'Dario, you may not have noticed, but we have a guest with us. This is Princess Shanna ...'

'I don't care if it's the Empress of China,' snarled Dario. 'You should have saved me some food.' He began to pace around the cell, his hands on his hips. 'Well, it's not good enough. I shall demand more food. I shall insist upon it!'

'Hey, calm down, big boy,' Princess Shanna advised him. 'You don't want to annoy those Draconians, they can be quite nasty when they put their minds to it.'

'Is that right?' Dario continued to glare at his brother. 'What did they give you?'

'Huh? Oh, just a meat pie. And to be honest, it wasn't that nice, it was something that the Princess couldn't eat. It was stone cold.'

'At least you ate *something*.' Dario sat down heavily on the bench next to his brother. He let out a long sigh. 'So what happens now?'

'I guess we go back to waiting,' said Mr Lazarus. He glanced at Princess Shanna. 'Hopefully Mr Stardancer will be here before very much longer.'

'Oh, I hope so,' said Princess Shanna. 'I really do.'

CHAPTER NINETEEN

The Rescue Party

The *Trillenium Hawk* came smoothly in to land on the planet Volpin Eight. Hunched at the controls, Blutacca hit a series of buttons and switches, then leaned back in his seat with a gruff sigh. There was a short silence. Then, as Kip and Stephanie watched, Zeke allowed his inner cloak to subside and he came gradually to his senses. When he was fully alert, he turned his head to one side and gazed at them.

'How did I do?' he asked dreamily.

'Brilliantly,' said Stephanie before Kip could respond. 'We got here without a single hitch. At one point, a Federation ship sailed right past us and didn't even know we were there. It was really exciting!'

Kip had to admit that the journey had been incredible but he couldn't help worrying that the available time to complete his mission was quickly running out.

'Excellent.' Zeke shook his head to dispel the last traces of the cloaking, then unbuckled his seatbelt and got to his feet. He flexed his shoulders and arms, then turned his attention to his Silonian co-pilot. 'Blooey, how far are we from the emperor's palace?'

'Snorgle drumple flex,' said Blutacca, pointing to his instrument panel.

'Hmm. That's quite some distance. But I see that we couldn't risk landing any closer, could we?'

'Sandge grolp,' said Blutacca, shaking his massive head.

Zeke thought for a moment. 'OK, my friends, let's work together. Blooey, you'll accompany me and Kip. We'll probably need your muscle power.'

'Wonga!' agreed Blutacca, looking pleased.

'Twerpy?'

'No, mistress?'

'You will stay here with Stephanie and look after the ship.'

'No way!' said Stephanie, unbuckling her own belt and getting to her feet. 'I'm not staying here, I want to go with you!'

Zeke stepped closer to her and placed a hand on her shoulder. 'The courage is strong in you,' he observed, 'and I commend that. But it could be

215

dangerous out there and it'll certainly be no place for a lady.'

'Oh, Zeke, really!' Stephanie looked at him scornfully. 'I'm not just a helpless female, you know. On my planet, I'm a reporter. I go into danger on a daily basis.'

Kip couldn't help thinking this was a bit of an exaggeration. Back in the village, the most dramatic thing she'd be expected to cover was a dispute about opening hours at the local community centre, but this probably wasn't the time to point that out to her.

Now Zeke looked confused. 'A reporter?' he murmured. 'But I thought you worked with Kip in the Rebel Alliance.'

'Er... yes, but only on a part-time basis. The rest of the time I work on a newspaper, the *Evening Post*. Maybe you've heard of it?'

'What's a *newspaper*?' asked Zeke.

'Never mind about all that,' said Kip impatiently. He got up from his own seat. 'We're wasting time. We need to get moving. And if Stephanie wants to come then that's up to her, surely?'

'Well, if you insist,' agreed Zeke. 'But I cannot say it gladdens me.' He clapped his hands together. 'All right then, the four of us will make up the rescue party. Let us prepare ourselves and dress for the mission.'

'Dress?' Kip gave him a wary look. 'What outfit would that be?'

Zeke grinned at him. 'You don't think we'd go out onto a hostile planet without weapons and armour, do you? Like I said, it could get rough out there. And it pays to be prepared.' He studied Kip doubtfully for a moment. 'I just hope we've got something in your size.'

★ ★ ★

Mr McCall was feeling very happy. He was sitting in the office counting the evening's takings, and with each hundred pounds that he put into the cashbox the more pleased he felt. It had been a long time since he'd taken over the reins of the Paramount and now, at last, thanks to Mr Lazarus and his amazing device, all those years of hard work and determination finally seemed to be paying off.

So intent was he on what he was doing, that it was a few moments before he realised that somebody was at the window of the ticket booth. He abandoned his counting and went to see what the man wanted. He was standing there, looking rather cross.

'If it's an ice cream you want, I'm afraid we've sold out,' said Dad. 'I've still got a few soft drinks left, if you want one.'

The man shook his head. He was thin, with a black moustache, and he was wearing a flat tweed cap. Now that Kip's dad was closer to him, he could see that the man was actually rather agitated. 'I do not want an ice cream or a soft drink,' he said flatly. 'What I've come here for is a refund.'

'A . . . refund?' This was unknown in his experience. 'But . . . aren't you enjoying the film?'

'No, I am not,' growled the man. 'In fact, I'd go so far as to say it's the biggest load of old rubbish I've ever seen in my life.'

Dad's mouth fell open. 'But . . . that's not a reason to ask for your money back,' he said. 'Just because you don't like the film. Anyway, what's wrong with it? The reviews have been good. Very good indeed.'

'What's wrong with it?' The man seemed outraged. 'What's *right* with it, you mean! I've seen all the other films in the series and they all made perfect sense – but this one is complete twaddle.

There are weird characters popping up out of nowhere who have nothing to do with the story. They're all saying nonsensical things . . . and weirdest of all, I'm sure I *know* some of them.'

'You . . . you *know* them? You mean . . .' Mr McCall broke off as it dawned on him that the man was obviously completely mad, possibly dangerous. The thing to do was to get him out of the cinema as quickly and quietly as possible. So, let him have his refund if that would speed things up. But just as he was reaching into the cashbox for the money, he heard a rising murmur of discontent from within the auditorium. The door swung open and more people, a woman and two young children came out, putting on their coats as they did so. The looks on their faces spoke louder than words ever could. The woman marched straight over to the window.

'I want my money back!' she said.

It began to dawn on him that something was horribly wrong . . . and that his long cherished moment of triumph looked to be teetering on the edge of a precipice.

★ ★ ★

Kip felt, once again, like a complete prat. Why was it that in every film he entered, he was expected to don some ridiculous outfit that had clearly been made for someone much bigger than him? The Alliance body armour was really cool, and under different circumstances he'd have been thrilled to try it on, but this outfit seemed to have been designed for somebody of Blutacca's dimensions. He'd somehow managed to struggle into the oversized space armour and the metal clad boots, but now Zeke was handing him a pulse rifle so big and heavy that he struggled to even lift it. Opposite him, Stephanie was at least tall enough for her outfit, but her skinny frame seemed lost beneath the white breastplate, shoulder pads and arm guards that Zeke had helped her put on and there was little chance that she'd be able to handle a large weapon. After a bit of rummaging, Zeke managed to come up with a dainty little pistol, which he pressed into her hands.

'There's not much stopping power in this,' he said, 'but it's better than nothing. Just remember to click off the safety catch before you pull the trigger.'

'What, this thing?' asked Stephanie; and an instant later, there was a loud hiss and a bright white beam of light shot out of the pistol and punched a hole in a breastplate that was hanging in a metal locker on the other side of the room.

'Whoah!' yelled Zeke. He leaned over and hastily snapped the catch back into position. 'Do not be too impetuous, fair lady! Let's just wait until you've got a Draconian in your sights before you do that again.'

'Sorry,' said Stephanie.

'It's OK. That suit needed repairing, anyway.'

Kip had just noticed something in a leather holster hanging at his side. He set down the rifle and pulled it free – a short wooden handle with a button on the side of it.

'Is this what I *think* it is?' he asked. He pressed the button and a straight beam of blue light shot upwards out of the handle to a height of four feet or so. 'Wow!' he said. 'It's a laser sword!'

'Yes,' said Zeke. 'And it's deadly, so watch what you do with it. The power is strong in you, Kip, but you have much to learn. When all this is over I shall take you to meet Master Scoda. He will teach you the ways of the Gredi.'

Kip was suddenly caught up in this incredible world. He could meet Scoda! The power was strong in him! He couldn't resist making a few flourishes with the weapon. It made a satisfying buzzing noise as he waved the beam around. But then he accidentally sliced the corner of a metal locker, as though it had no more substance than a block of butter and a stern look from Zeke bought him back to reality – or what passed for reality at the moment.

He switched off the device and returned it to its holster. 'Are we ready to go?' he asked, trying to move things along.

'Blooey?' called Zeke, and almost immediately the Silonian appeared, wearing no armour at all and carrying a weapon that made Kip's pulse rifle look positively titchy by comparison. Crisscrossed on his mighty chest, he wore two leather bandoliers that were filled with some kind of ammunition – bullets that emitted a ghastly green glow.

'Greedlethip wonga tango Draco bang!' he roared, punching the air with one mighty fist. It probably meant something like, 'Let's go and kick some Draconian butt.' He led the way towards an exit and thumped a button on the wall as he passed. The metal hatch slid aside to reveal that it was nighttime on Volpin Eight and, in the cold moonlight, Kip could see a vista of grim, rocky terrain, not dissimilar to what he had encountered on Tarka Daal. He instantly felt edgy. The reduced visibility was not something he had expected. Blutacca strode eagerly down the ramp, his weapon held ready to fire, and Zeke and Stephanie followed a little more cautiously. Kip reluctantly brought up the rear.

'Hello!' shouted a monotone voice behind him and Kip glanced over his shoulder to see T-Twerpio standing in the open hatchway, waving a hand at them. 'Be very concerned,' he shouted. 'I'll take terrible care of the *Millennium Hippo* while you're here!'

Kip shook his head. T-Twerpio's back-to-front chatter still took some getting used to. He stepped off the ramp onto the hard rocky earth and followed Zeke and Stephanie, his muscles already aching from the weight of the pulse rifle cradled in his arms. As he walked, he kept sweeping his gaze from left to right and back again, reluctant to run unprepared into anything as extreme as he had on his last visit to an unfamiliar planet. But, as far as he could see, there were no signs of life, just a rolling landscape of jagged hills and tumbled rocks that seemed to stretch for miles in every direction.

As they walked, Stephanie directed an endless stream of questions at Zeke.

'Where are we?'

'A planet called Volpin Eight.'

'And why are we here, exactly?'

'Because this is where the Emperor Zarkan has bought the hostages. We're going to attempt to rescue them.'

'I see. And . . . these hostages? One of them must be this Princess Shanna, I suppose?'

'Well, yes, that's right. I can't very well leave her in the grip of an evil dictator, can I?'

There was a long silence as though Stephanie were considering her answer. When she finally spoke, her voice was surly and resentful, like a spoiled child. 'I suppose when you see her, you'll remember why you fell in love with her in the first place and then you'll want to be with her all over again.'

Zeke didn't seem to know how to answer this so Kip broke in, trying to help him out.

'There's Mr L— There's Barty Skythump too,' he reminded her. 'And his brother. They also need rescuing.'

'Oh yes, the mysterious Mr Skythump,' said Stephanie, making no attempt to hide the sarcasm in her voice. 'The reason why we're here in the first place. I'll certainly have a few harsh words for him when we find him.'

'Drunkle thumpa tingle sweep!' warned Blutacca, pointing, and everybody lifted their heads to see what the problem was. Kip saw that the way ahead passed through a narrow ravine. High cliffs rose sheer on either side of them.

'Blooey says this looks like a perfect place for an ambush,' observed Zeke. 'But it'd take weeks to find a way around it.' He looked first at Stephanie and then at Kip. 'I vote we go ahead. Blooey?'

'Yowsa!'

'Stephanie?'

'Agreed!' said Stephanie, without hesitation.

'Kip?'

'Er . . . whatever.' He was beginning to wish that he'd stayed on the ship with T-Twerpio. Not that it had ever been an option. He couldn't help feeling that there wasn't much time left to find Mr Lazarus.

'OK.' Zeke gestured to Blutacca to continue and the Silonian shrugged his massive shoulders and continued on his way.

They moved on in single file and Kip felt the massive shadows of the ravine close around him, cutting off the air and making everything, even their footsteps, sound hollow and unreal. Just then, with a suddenness that made him jump, his phone began to ring and he spent a bit of time rooting about under his armour to fish it out of his jeans pocket. He lifted it to his ear. 'Hi, Beth,' he said warily.

'Kip, you need to get back here now!' Beth sounded frantic. 'Half the audience is getting up to leave, and I'm expecting your dad to turn up at any moment to ask what's going on. What am I supposed to tell him?'

'I don't know,' he said wearily. 'Tell him . . .'

'Yes?'

'Tell him that I'm on a planet called Volpin Eight and I'm trying to find Mr Lazarus.'

'Oh well, thanks for that. Yeah, I'm sure that will go down very well.' A baffled pause, then, 'Oh, and, Kip?'

'Yes?'

'I hate to say this, but that creepy music is starting again.'

'You're kidding!'

'I wish.'

'Look, the battery on my phone is nearly down,

so maybe you'd better ring off now – but call me again if anything new happens.'

'I will. Take care out there.'

Beth rang off and Kip continued to look around, but now he could only see as far as the sheer walls of rock that rose up on either side of him. It was a horrible, claustrophobic feeling. 'Zeke!' he yelled and his voice seemed to echo eerily in the confined space.

'Yes?'

'I've... I've just had a tip-off that something bad might be about to happen.'

'Really? Something like what?'

'I don't know, exactly. My... er... my contact says she can hear creepy music, so...'

Zeke actually stopped walking and turned back to face Kip. 'Did I hear you right? Your contact can hear *music*? Is that what you said?'

'Yes and it's a sign that something bad is going to happen. I can't explain, but the last time she heard it, that thing came up out of the lake on Tarka Daal and I nearly got eaten.'

'But... music? That doesn't make any sense.'

'Oh yes, it does,' said Kip. 'Just take my word for it.'

'Well, we can't turn back now. We'll have to press on until we reach the—' The rest of Zeke's words were obliterated by a shrill, whining sound that seemed to come from the air high above them. Kip tilted his head to look towards the sky and saw a trail of white light descending through the star-strewn heavens, looking as though it would fall to earth some distance in front of them. He pointed. 'What's that?' he asked.

'Hit the dirt!' yelled Zeke. He grabbed Stephanie and pulled her to the ground with him, behind the big, shaggy shape of Blutacca, who was already following the order. Kip opened his mouth to ask something else but then the earth beneath him seemed to ripple like a rocky carpet and a blast of hot air struck him in the chest and lifted him clean off his feet. He was vaguely aware of a great blossoming of orange flame almost twenty metres in front of him and briefly felt the heat of it on his face – but then he was propelled backwards for quite some distance, before his backside connected with the ground and he came to a painful, skidding halt. He sat there, looking open-mouthed at the others, who were now quite a way ahead of him, silhouetted in front of the flames. He saw Blutacca and Zeke getting back to their feet, their pulse rifles flinging beams of yellow light up towards the top of the cliff to their left. When Kip turned his head to look, he saw movement up there, white armoured space troopers, firing back at the people below, their own laser blasts arcing down and flinging up great explosions of stone and dirt in all directions. Blutacca had been right. It *was* the perfect place for an ambush.

Now Stephanie was on her feet too, firing the pistol in all directions and blasting great chunks out of the cliff walls, which was no help to anybody.

Kip snatched in a breath and scrambled upright. He brought his own rifle round to train the sights on those moving figures and he squeezed the trigger, but absolutely nothing happened. He remembered what Zeke had said about the safety catch and he fumbled with the trigger, trying to find it. More by luck than design, he managed to flick something to one side with a harsh click. Almost instantly, his gun spewed fire, the impact pushing the weapon hard against his shoulder. He lost his footing and went down on his back, still firing, the pulse rifle discharging its payload pointlessly into the sky. He remembered to stop squeezing the trigger and struggled back into a sitting position.

Another explosion to his right knocked him sideways. Dirt and pebbles rained down on his head, flinging dust into his eyes. He cursed, staggered back to his feet and stumbled forward, trying to locate the others, but he had only a glimpse of a white-clothed figure, running through a maelstrom of swirling dust, shooting arcs of flame into the air above him. And then, Kip became aware of a noise in the sky, not the high-pitched sound he'd heard before, but a low, ominous rumble. He coughed, wiped the dust from his eyes with his sleeve and looked upwards, to see a dark oval mass hovering in the sky above the ravine – a dark shape that suddenly burst into glaring, white light, the power of it searing his eyes. He lifted the rifle to fire at the shape but something came rushing down through the intervening space, something like a huge metal hand on the end of a long cable, and the fingers of the hand closed around the barrel of the gun and wrenched it out of Kip's grasp, flinging it aside like a useless twig.

Kip took the hint and turned to run, heading back the way he had come, telling himself that if he could just make it back as far the *Trillenium Hawk* he could get more weapons, come back for another attempt ... but, even as the thought leaped and twisted through his mind, he felt a jarring impact as something slammed into his back and then what felt like giant fingers closed around his shoulders, pinning his arms to his sides. He tried to struggle but the power in those metal fingers was awesome and he could only wriggle and squirm where he stood, before the arm was suddenly retracted and he was pulled upwards at unbelievable speed, cold wind rushing past him as he rocketed through the empty air. It occurred to him that he might be about to die and he groped for the handle of the laser sword as he rushed upwards through the air. If he could just pull it free...

Another impact shook him to his very core and the metal fingers suddenly relaxed their grip. He fully expected to fall back to earth, but instead found himself tumbling sideways, headlong into some kind of metal mesh container. He slammed up against a warm, furry shape, a shape that was squirming and bellowing at an ear-splitting volume and he registered that it was Blutacca. But even as the thought occurred to him, something hard and heavy caught him a glancing blow to the side of the head and everything dissolved in to a whirling, melting confusion of noises and smells.

Then a darkness welled up within him, a darkness that tasted like something he'd been given at the dentist when he was very small, and it was as though his limbs had lost all power to function and he could do nothing but give in and slide silently into darkness.

CHAPTER TWENTY

Captives

Mr McCall was absolutely horrified. He stood there in the small office, experiencing a terrible sinking sensation in the pit of his stomach, because now the door to the auditorium had swung open again and he could see that scores of customers were coming out, pulling on their coats and shaking their heads and looking as if they were about ready to lynch somebody.

He was obliged to come out of the office, into the foyer, holding up his hands in an attempt to appease the crowd and try to gauge exactly what the problem was, but everybody seemed to be talking at once.

'Never seen anything so stupid in my...'

'...rubbish! I don't know how they've got the cheek to charge money to...'

'...swear one of them is that drippy woman who works for the local...'

'...I could write better dialogue myself!'

233

'Please,' he cried. 'One at a time! I can't under-stand what the problem is.'

'The problem is it's a terrible film,' said the man in the flat cap. 'Absolute nonsense. I kept thinking it might improve, but if anything it's getting worse.'

'Well,' said Kip's dad, 'perhaps we could—'

But he broke off as a familiar figure hurried out of the cinema, pushing and barging his way through the others. It was Norman and his normally ruddy features were pale and drawn, as though he'd had some kind of a shock.

'Norman?' murmured Mr McCall, feeling some-what betrayed. 'You didn't even pay for *your* seat.'

Norman shook his head and jerked a thumb over his shoulder, towards the door of the auditorium. 'It . . . it's Kip!' he gasped.

'Kip? What's wrong with him?'

'He's just been blown up by aliens,' said Norman and Dad felt as though the floor had been jerked from under his feet.

He stared at Norman in disbelief. 'He's been *what*?' he cried. Had Norman gone completely barmy? Living with Kitty probably wasn't much fun, but it was no excuse for this kind of madness. 'Have you been drinking or something?'

'I know how it sounds,' gasped Norman. 'But I saw him, I did, up on the screen. I didn't believe it at first, I thought it must have been somebody who *looked* like him, but when he started talking I knew it was definitely him. He was with Zeke Stardancer and . . . and that reporter from the local paper.'

'Stephanie?'

'Yes. I don't understand it, but I know Kip when I see him, and he was there, as though he was part of the film. And then there were all these explosions and the next thing I knew he was flying through the air . . .'

But Mr McCall was already pushing through the crowd towards the auditorium doors, ignoring the audience's demands for money, intent now on only one thing: checking that his son was OK.

★ ★ ★

Kip opened his eyes to find a whole crowd of people standing over him. He recognised Mr Lazarus's face and smiled up at him in relief.

'Are you all right?' the old man asked.

'I'm fine . . . I think,' said Kip. He patted his body carefully, trying to determine if anything were broken but, as far as he could tell, it was all intact. He noticed that his body armour was gone and he was back in the T-shirt and jeans he'd been wearing under it. The laser sword was gone too and, when he slipped a hand into the pocket of his jeans, his mobile phone was missing as well. He glanced round quickly and determined that he was in some kind of windowless cell. There was quite a crowd in there with him: Dario, Stephanie, the big shambling shape of Blutacca and, he was surprised to note, Princess Shanna. They were all huddled in a corner, talking agitatedly amongst themselves. He returned his attention to Mr Lazarus. 'Where are we?' he asked.

'In the emperor's palace,' said Mr Lazarus. 'Or at least, its cells.'

'And . . . where's Zeke?'

'That's what we were gonna ask *you*,' said an imperious American voice and Princess Shanna strode across the cell to stand over him. 'This woman . . .' She pointed to Stephanie. 'This woman claims to have been with him when you were all attacked.'

'Er . . . yeah, that's right,' said Kip, trying not to stare at her. She was every bit as gorgeous in real life as she was on the screen. 'We were making our way here and we were ambushed by the emperor's troopers.'

'So what happened to Zeke?' asked Princess Shanna.

'I told you,' said Stephanie. 'I saw him running up the ravine. He was firing at something. That was just before that big hand thingy grabbed me. Then there was an explosion and . . .' She spread her hands. 'I didn't see him again, after that.'

Princess Shanna frowned. 'There's always hope,' she said. 'Until they show me his still and broken body, there's a chance that he's alive. Zeke is a survivor. A hundred times the emperor has had him backed into a corner and against all the odds, he's fought his way out. That's why he's the man that I love.'

There was a silence and then Dario said, 'I don't suppose anybody's got any food on them?' Everyone looked at him, outraged by his insensitivity. 'Well, excuse me,' he said. 'I only asked.'

Princess Shanna moved back across the cell and started talking to Blutacca in hushed tones.

Mr Lazarus smiled at Kip. 'It was good of you to come in after me,' he said. 'Especially after everything you said.'

'That's OK,' whispered Kip. 'I even had a laser sword, but they must have taken it from me when I was knocked out. Sorry.'

Mr Lazarus smiled. 'Oh, that's all right,' he said. 'I think we have other things to worry about, right now.'

Kip leaned closer so he could whisper. 'But there's no need to worry, is there?' he said. 'We can leave now. Just get Dario and Stephanie to come over here and we'll be on our way.'

'And leave the Princess and Blutacca locked up here?'

'Oh, don't worry about them, I know how these films work. Zeke is sure to be along in a while and rescue them. And we don't have a lot of time left.' He slipped a hand beneath his T-shirt to get the Retriever and his fingers found nothing at all. A horrible realisation dawned, making his stomach lurch. 'Oh, no,' he whispered.

Mr Lazarus looked at him, puzzled. 'What's the matter?' he asked.

'The Retriever,' said Kip forlornly. 'It's gone.'

★ ★ ★

Jambo Jinks hurried along the corridor with the strange flashing pendant clutched in both hands. It had been hanging around the neck of one of the new captives and though he wasn't sure exactly what it was, it looked as though it might be important — a weapon, perhaps, or some means of communication. Whatever it was, the emperor was sure to want to know about it and, after his humiliation in front of Commander Skelp, this seemed like the perfect opportunity for Jinks to get back in the emperor's good books. Perhaps then he might be more willing to listen to Jinks's request for the hand of Princess Shanna in marriage.

Oh, he knew that they had little in common, but he was convinced that once she'd seen his cosy little villa on Volpin Eight and had realised what an important fellow he was, she'd soon come round to the old Jinks magic. He'd be a much better catch than some semi-literate farm boy with a hero complex, at any rate.

Jinks paused outside the massive wooden doors of the emperor's room and tapped politely. There was a long silence, before an irritated voice asked, 'Who is it?'

'It is I, Your Magnificence,' said Jinks, using the

oiliest tone possible. 'Your faithful servant, Jambo Jinks.'

'What do *you* want?' asked the emperor. He didn't sound in the best of moods, but that wasn't unusual.

'Begging your Majesty's pardon, but a skirmish party just came in with several captives. One of them had something upon his person that I thought you might want to see.'

There was a long sigh and then a silence. 'Oh, very well,' said the emperor at last, and then the doors opened silently, seemingly of their own accord. There stood the emperor in the centre of the room. He was cloaked as ever, his pale eyes burning in the shadow of his hood. 'This had better be good,' he warned. 'I was just about to watch *The Universe Has Talent.*'

'Your Incredibleness.' Jinks entered the room, bowed low and proffered the flashing pendant to his employer.

'What's this?' murmured Zarkan. He extended a wizened hand and picked the device up by its chain, allowing it to swing to and fro in front of his gaze. 'Looks like something you'd pick up in a rocket-boot sale.'

'Alas, I've no idea *what* it is, Your Majesty. But it looked important. It was hung around the neck of a boy.'

'A boy?'

'Yes, Your Graciousness. He's down in the cells with the other captives – a woman and the Silonian who calls himself Blutacca.'

That got the emperor's attention, just as Jinks had known it would. 'Blutacca? But he's the co-pilot of—'

'Yes, Your Eminence,' said Jinks, relishing his tiny triumph. 'Stardancer! The leader of the Rebel Alliance and the man who the prophecy says will one day rule the universe! Now his co-pilot is our prisoner... and several troopers claim to have seen Stardancer during the skirmish, just before...'

'Before what?' asked Zarkan suspiciously.

'Before he escaped, Sire. But don't despair. Our best men are out right now, attempting to track him down. It's only a matter of time before they bring him in.'

'Hmm.' The emperor was clearly unconvinced. 'Seems to me I've heard that somewhere before.' He considered the Retriever for a moment. 'Tell me about this... boy,' he said.

'Just a young whelp, perhaps some twelve or thirteen years of age, dressed in Rebel Alliance space armour that was much too big for him. An earthling, I believe, the same as the previous two captives we brought in. I shouldn't be at all surprised if they are connected in some way.'

'Interesting,' said the emperor. He lifted the Retriever to take a closer look at it and, with one thumb, he unlatched the metal cover to reveal the flashing red 'eject' button. 'What am I to make of this?' he mused. 'What can it mean?' He placed a thumb on the button. 'Am I supposed to press it? And what happens if I do?'

'Be careful, Your Majesty! What if it's some kind of weapon?'

'Entrusted to a young boy? It was around his neck, you say?'

'Yes, my Lord. Hidden beneath his armour, as though he wanted to keep it safe.'

'And what would such a word indicate? Eject? To remove. To escape.' His hooded head nodded. 'I believe this is some kind of transportation device. A way of moving between worlds. Perhaps this is how the Rebel Alliance planned to assassinate me. To send a killer into my realm. And perhaps...

perhaps that young boy is the assassin.'

'An assassin, Your Highness? But he's just a youngster!'

'What better cover for a ruthless killer, Jinks? Think of it! Who would suspect one so young? He could easily have bluffed his way close enough to me to strike a fatal blow. It's only by chance that he and his accomplices were intercepted. Of course, what his masters won't be expecting is for me to use their own means of transportation to catch them in their lair. Why don't I go straight to them and take my revenge? I'll nip this little plan in the bud.'

'By yourself, Your Majesty? Excuse me, but is that wise? Perhaps if you took a detachment of space troopers with you . . .'

'You doubt my power, Jinks? You think I need somebody to back me up?'

'Oh, no, Your . . . Your Excellency. I just . . .'

'I have been dealing with people like this since I was a young boy myself.'

'I'm sure. I only . . .'

'Watch, Jinks. Watch and learn how a true leader takes command of a situation!'

He pressed the button with his thumb. For a

moment, his cloaked figure seemed to shimmer like a cluster of stars. And then, quite suddenly, he was gone.

'Your Fabulousness?' whispered Jinks. 'Hello? Yoo hoo?' Jinks looked around the room. He was completely alone. 'Now, where in the world did he go?' he muttered.

CHAPTER TWENTY-ONE

A Visitor

Looking at the screen, Beth saw what was about to happen and spun round to face the Enigma in absolute horror. But even as she turned, the platform was glowing with an unearthly white light, sliding to the end of its track and . . . quite suddenly, there was Emperor Zarkan, standing on the wooden platform, looking around the tiny projection room in astonishment, the Retriever still clutched in one bony hand.

Rose screamed and Beth acted instinctively, realising that the one chance she had of banishing the most evil man in the Universe from the projection room of the Paramount Picture Palace, was to push him straight back into the light. But as she lunged forward, the emperor's free hand lifted, fist clenched, and from the ring on his finger an eerie purple ray erupted, bathing Beth in its glow and rooting her to the spot, arms outstretched, her face frozen in a grimace of dismay.

Rose stared up at Beth in absolute horror. She reached up and pulled at Beth's T-shirt, but she was completely rigid.

'You've frozen her!' gasped Rose. 'There was no need for that.'

'Of course there was,' the emperor corrected her, stepping down from the platform. 'She was trying to attack me.'

'Was *not*!' said Rose grumpily. 'She was only trying to send you back. You're not supposed to be here.' She stared up at Beth's horrified face. 'Unfreeze her,' she demanded.

'No,' said the emperor, in his horrible sigh of a voice. 'Now, tell me everything you know about your plans for my assassination.'

'My plans for what?' Rose stared at him blankly.

'Come, come, you know what I'm talking about. I've caught you red-handed, right here in your headquarters.' He gazed around the room. 'Where *is* this place?' he asked.

'It's the Paramount Picture Palace,' said Rose. 'But you shouldn't be here, you're supposed to be in the film.'

The emperor stared down at her. 'What film?' he croaked.

'*Space Blasters*, you numpty! You're supposed to be the villain. Don't you know that?'

'I haven't the faintest idea what you're on about,' said the Emperor. 'What planet is this?'

'It's Earth, of course.' Rose reached up and tried pulling at one of Beth's arms, but it was stiff and unyielding. 'You sure she'll be all right?' Rose asked. She'd seen this done to both Jambo Jinks and Dario in the film, so she knew the effect was only temporary, but that didn't stop it from feeling weird.

'Yes, yes. Stop nagging or you'll join her! So, we're on Earth. And you're part of the plot to assassinate me.'

'No, I'm not,' said Rose huffily. 'I'm Kip's sister.'

'Kip? Who's Kip?'

'My brother.'

'Yes, *obviously*! And this is your headquarters? The place where you plan your fiendish schemes?'

'No. This is the Paramount. You're here because you pressed the eject button.' She pointed to the glowing device still held in the Emperor's hand. 'It brought you out of the film, didn't it?'

'Film?' The emperor still wasn't getting it. 'You keep saying that word. What film?'

'*That* one,' snapped Rose irritably. She pointed to the viewing hatch, thinking to herself that for an emperor this guy really was a bit dim. He moved slowly towards it and peered through. Then he said something really rude. Onscreen, there was a long shot of his palace on Volpin Eight. Thousands of people were gathered in the courtyard, as if for a special event. Then the camera tracked in on a balcony at the front of the palace, and as Zarkan watched in disbelief, a familiar insect-headed figure strode out of the shadows and stood there, surveying the crowd, his compound eyes flashing in the sunlight. It was just possible to make out what he was saying. 'The emperor is dead!' he announced. 'Long live the emperor!' And the crowd began to cheer.

'What the . . . ?' Zarkan reacted as though he'd just been hit with an electric prod. He moved to the door, threw it open and hurried outside.

'Wait!' cried Rose, hurrying after him. 'You're not allowed to go out there.'

The emperor found himself in the midst of chaos. Hundreds of people were sitting all around him, shouting and complaining, some of them throwing rubbish in the general direction of the screen.

Clearly they disliked Jinks as much as the emperor did. As he began to glide down the stairs, they reacted with general disbelief, pointing and laughing at him, showing no respect whatsoever. Irritated, he lifted his ring hand and directed a great sweeping arc of light around the room, freezing whole groups of people into sudden immobility. The emperor didn't hesitate, he moved on down the stairs, his arm sweeping left and right to silence anyone who made a noise or a movement. His only interest was to get closer to the screen to hear what Jinks was saying. Pretty soon, nearly all the people in the seats were still and silent, expressions of complete surprise on their faces. Others were frozen in the act of getting up and putting their coats on. He even noticed two Federation troopers in their distinctive white armour, immobilised with the rest of them, and thought to himself that they might have come in useful, though he couldn't imagine how they had got here before him. Traitors, perhaps? Double agents?

As the emperor neared the bottom of the steps, the entrance doors burst open and a man ran into the room, pursued by an angry mob. He turned to head up the stairs towards the projection room, then stopped, mouth open, staring at the approaching figure of the emperor. The pursuing mob closed in on him angrily and one creature, wearing a flat cap, glanced at the emperor and then shouted, 'Don't think a cheap publicity stunt like this is going to stop me from getting my money back!' The emperor silenced the entire group with a blast of purple light and then moved past them until he was approaching the screen itself.

A last few people blundered in through the entrance doors as he reached the bottom of the steps and he froze them without even looking at them. Finally, the place was silent enough for him to hear what Jinks was actually saying, up on the screen, as he spoke to the gathered masses of Volpin Eight.

'. . . as you know, it's now been three weeks since Emperor Zarkan's mysterious disappearance . . .'

'Three weeks?' hissed the emperor. 'But . . . I only left a few moments ago!'

'That happens,' said a voice behind him and he turned to see the little girl standing there. She was holding something up, a little oblong box. It flashed with a bright white light, momentarily dazzling him.

'What did you just do?' he growled.

'I just took a photograph,' said the girl and she slipped the box back into her pocket. 'But about the time thing. Beth calls it, "edited highlights". She says you could be in there a hundred years, but on the screen it only seems like five minutes.' She pointed back up the aisle. 'Is my daddy going to be all right? Only you froze him too on your way down the stairs.'

'Oh, do shut up, he's going to be fine. Now let me concentrate on what that idiot is saying!'

The emperor returned his attention to Jinks, who continued with his speech. '. . . must now accept that all hope is gone. Luckily, we have taken captive the earthlings who caused the emperor's disappearance and before much longer, they will be made to pay for their evil deeds. In the meantime, of course, there is the emperor's will to consider. . .' He held up a scroll of paper and waved it at the crowd. '. . . which was found amongst his personal effects. And you also know that in this will, he names me as his natural successor. . .'

The emperor made a choking sound.

'Are you all right?' asked Rose, stepping closer, but he waved her to silence. He was leaning forward now, as though afraid of missing a single word of what Jinks was saying.

'And so it is with heavy heart that I accept this awesome responsibility, in the sure and certain knowledge that this is what the emperor himself would have wanted me to do.'

'Why, that lying little worm!' The emperor's hands bunched into fists. 'What *will*? I never left a will. And even if I had, I wouldn't have chosen him as a successor if he was the last creature left in the galaxy.'

'And so, I reluctantly and humbly accept the position of Emperor of the Universe and pledge myself to serve the people of Volpin Eight to the best of my ability. I may have the head of an insect, but I have the blood and the heart of a warrior. And since I don't really suit a hood, due to my rather large cranium, I have decided to make a small change to the ceremony.' He clapped his hands and Princess Shanna walked out onto the balcony, carrying a velvet cushion on which sat a golden crown, glittering with multicoloured precious jewels. This would have looked more convincing if the princess hadn't been escorted by Commander Skelp, who was quite clearly pushing something into her back, most probably a pulse pistol. The princess stepped up to Jinks, lifted the crown from the cushion and placed it, none too gently, onto his head. The crowd in the courtyard below applauded loudly.

Jinks waited for the applause to die down then continued. 'As my first act as your emperor, it gives me great pleasure to announce a Royal Wedding! Yes, people of Volpin Eight, I'm happy to announce that Princess Shanna has agreed to become Empress of the Universe and rule by my side.'

At this there was more cheering from the crowd, but Zarkan clearly didn't feel like joining in.

'The scheming little space rat,' he snarled. 'If he marries the princess then he will in effect be making a peace treaty with the Alliance. I can't allow that! They're my mortal enemies.' He wheeled round and glared down at Rose. 'I have to go back,' he said. 'I must prevent this from happening.' He looked at the pendant in his hand and tried pushing the button, but absolutely nothing happened. Rose looked at him scornfully.

'That only works when you're in there,' she said, pointing to the screen.

'Well then, tell me how I can go back,' snapped the emperor. 'Quickly, girl, there isn't any time to waste.'

Rose scowled. She turned round and looked at

the cinema behind her, the seats packed with people all frozen in whatever attitude they'd been in when the ray had hit them. It was an uncanny sight. 'What about this lot?' she asked.

The emperor waved a hand. 'That's nothing,' he assured her. 'I told you, in half an hour or so, they'll come back to their senses and be just as they were before. Which is frankly not saying much for them. Now, come on, stop wasting my time. Can you or can you not send me back to Volpin Eight?'

'I can,' said Rose warily. 'But first you have to promise to do something for me.'

The emperor's amber eyes seemed to blaze with anger. 'You dare to impose conditions on me?' he hissed. 'I am the Emperor of the Universe!'

'No you're not,' said Rose. She pointed to the screen where Jinks was now parading down a street, arm-in-arm with a reluctant-looking Princess Shanna. '*He* is,' she said.

'But . . . he lied to my people! He told them I was dead.'

'And you may as well be, if I don't send you back there.'

'Why, you—' The emperor lifted his hand to unleash the freezing ray but Rose shook her head.

'I wouldn't do that I were you,' she said. 'If you freeze me, I won't be able to help you, will I? And if the film finishes before you get back into it, you'll never ever be able to go there again.'

'What, *never*?'

'Never. You'll be stuck here.' She glanced quickly round the room. 'And I don't think you'd like that.'

The emperor let out a long sigh. 'Oh, very well,' he snapped. 'Tell me your condition.'

Rose nodded. 'When you get back there . . .' She pointed at the screen. 'You've got to give that' – she gestured at the Retriever in the emperor's hand – 'to my brother, Kip.'

'And who might that be?'

'He's a friend of Zeke Stardancer. He had the Retriever hanging around his neck. He's now in a cell in your palace.'

'Ah, yes, Jinks spoke of a boy just before I pressed the button. Yes, very well, I'll see that he gets it. Now can we . . . ?'

'You have to *promise*!' insisted Rose.

'Don't you trust me?'

'No, I do not. You're the baddie, you always lie about stuff.'

'Well, really! I'll have you know, I'm famous

throughout the Universe for never going back on what I say.'

'Good. Then you won't mind promising, will you?'

'Time is slipping away, girl!'

'I know. So you'd better promise quickly, hadn't you?'

'Oh . . . very well! I . . . I promise.'

'You promise what?'

'That I'll give this thing . . .' The emperor shook the Retriever ' . . . to your brother, Kit.'

'Kip!'

'Yes, to your brother, Kip. Now do we have a deal or not?'

'I suppose so . . .' Rose turned and started back towards the steps.

'Where are you going?'

'Back to the projection room, of course. That's where we'll send you from. Are you coming or what?'

The emperor followed her and the two of them made their way through the groups of frozen figures crowded on the steps.

Rose indicated the man who had been pursued by an angry crowd. 'That's my dad,' she said. 'He owns this place.'

'Lucky him,' said the emperor. 'Tell me, are all the little girls on earth like you?'

'Oh, no,' Rose assured him. 'I'm special. My dad always says I'm a proper little madam.'

'Hmm. He's obviously an excellent judge of character.'

They reached the top of the stairs and went into the projection room. Beth was still exactly as she had been when they left, transfixed in a running position, her arms out in front of her. Rose looked at her for a moment. 'One other thing,' she said. 'My friend, Beth.'

'What about her?'

'I want you to wake her up.'

'I thought I told you – that will happen anyway.'

'You don't get it. You need both of us to send you back. So you'd better fix her.'

'But . . .'

'NOW!'

Zarkan muttered something under his breath, but he lifted his hand and pointed the gold ring at Beth. He seemed to concentrate very hard and then she was bathed in a pink light. She stirred, stumbled, almost fell. Then she stood there, blinking around the room, looking confused.

'What . . . what happened?' she gasped.

'Nothing much.' Rose indicated Zarkan. 'You got frozen by him. So did the audience.' She pointed at the emperor. 'He needs to go back into the film. I said we'd send him.'

'But . . . that's Zarkan. The most evil man in the Universe.' Beth blearily indicated the Perspex device, dangling from one of his hands. 'And . . . he's got the Retriever!'

'Yes, I know. He's going to give it to Kip just as soon as he gets back in the film.'

'Er . . . OK. But . . . can we trust him to do that?'

'I think so,' said Rose. 'He promised and everything. And he can't break a promise.' She looked at the Emperor sternly. 'If he does, we'll just bring him straight back here, won't we, Beth?'

'Er . . . yes, we will.'

'And then he can just be emperor of this?' She waved a hand around the room.

The emperor studied them for a moment. 'I doubt that you *can* bring me back,' he said. 'Surely it requires me to press the button when I'm in there.'

'That's for us to know and you to find out,' said Beth darkly.

'Yeah,' said Rose. 'Big time.' She indicated the wooden platform. 'Right,' she said. 'Get on.'

'As simple as that?' cried the emperor, dismayed. 'I would have figured that out for myself, sooner or later.'

'Yes, but what's tricky is keeping an eye on the film, looking for just the right place to send you back in.' She looked at Beth. 'Isn't that right?'

'Er...absolutely,' said Beth, still trying to make her brain understand what had happened while she'd been 'gone'. 'Yeah, if we get it wrong, you'll be sorry you ever came out.' She made herself move to the viewing window. 'Er...climb on, Your ...Your Majesty,' she said. She watched as the emperor stepped up onto the wooden platform. 'Now. Where er...where exactly do you want to be when you arrive?'

'Near that little rat, Jinks,' snarled the emperor. 'Preferably within punching distance.'

'OK.' Beth shook her head to clear the last traces of fog from it. Then she nodded to Rose, who lifted a foot and placed it on the platform. 'Get ready,' said Beth. 'I'll count you in.' And she turned her head to look at the screen.

CHAPTER TWENTY-TWO

The Wedding

Jinks studied himself in the full-length mirror, and decided that all things considered, he was a fine figure of an insectoid. The most skilled tailors on Volpin Eight had created his wedding outfit, an elegant black suit, which he wore with a frilly white shirt and a crimson silk sash wound tightly around his rather podgy waist. The problem was, he'd been letting himself go a bit lately, eating whatever food was put in front of him and demanding seconds, so the suit was already pinching him in half a dozen places. He told himself that once he was a married man, he wouldn't have to worry about that. He'd sit around in his underwear all day, eating salt 'n' vinegar earthworms and drinking nectar to his heart's content.

'How do I look?' he asked Commander Skelp, who was standing a short distance away with a disapproving look on his lizardy face.

'Very... distinguished,' said Skelp, trying to mask his evident dislike of Jinks, but no doubt realising that it wouldn't be wise to fall out with the new Emperor of the Universe.

'Listen,' said Jinks. 'I'm as cut up about the disappearance of Zarkan as you, but we have to put a brave face on it. He wouldn't want us to sit around moping, would he? If he were here now, he'd be applauding this marriage.'

'If he were here now,' said Skelp drily, 'he'd still be emperor.'

'Er... yes, I suppose that's true... but he's gone. We have to accept that. And he wouldn't have written that will leaving everything to me, if he didn't want me to take his place, would he?'

'I suppose not. It was quite convenient, wasn't it, you finding the will so quickly after his disappearance?'

'Hmm.' Jinks turned and studied Skelp for a moment. 'It was a complete surprise to me. But just a measure, I believe, of how much the emperor valued my services. I've been thinking, Commander Skelp, that once I'm married I'll be in need of somebody to take total control of Volpin Eight's fighting forces. I think *General* Skelp has a nice ring to it, does it not? It also carries a much bigger salary.'

Skelp bowed his head. 'Your er . . . Your Majesty is most generous,' he said meekly.

'Not at all. After all, it's only what Emperor Zarkan would have wanted.' Jinks turned back to the mirror and made a few more small adjustments to his outfit. 'Now, Commander, give me the run down on today's joyful proceedings.'

'Of course, Your Majesty. Well, as you already know, the wedding will take place at ten hundred hours prompt in the great cathedral. Your union will be witnessed by all the most prosperous citizens of Volpin Eight. The captives will also be brought along to witness the event – in chains, of course – and directly afterwards, they'll be taken to the arena. I thought that rather than feed them to the wild beasts, as the previous emperor would have done, we'd give proceedings a family day out sort of feel with fireworks and a communal barbecue. There are four earthlings and a Silonian, so there should be plenty to go around.'

'Excellent. Sounds like my idea of fun! And what of Princess Shanna?'

'She's currently being prepared for the wedding, Your Majesty. I er . . . took the precaution of administering her a dose of Zallium, this morning.

It will calm her down, make her more... compliant.'

Jinks sighed. 'It's a shame she can't enter more into the spirit of the occasion,' he said. 'I've given her jewels, fine clothes, the best food... what more does she want?'

Skelp shrugged his shoulders. 'I rather fear she's holding out hope that Stardancer may yet come to her aid.'

'Stardancer? Hah! There's little chance of that. My troops have scoured every inch of this planet and found no trace of him. He was clearly blown to atoms in the attack. But, just as a precaution, make sure that a double guard is placed around the cathedral. We don't want anything to mar this special day, do we?'

'No, your Majesty.'

Jinks reached to a table alongside him where, on its velvet cushion, his crown rested, glittering magnificently in the morning sunlight. He ran a finger lovingly over its layers of precious jewels. He'd had the finest craftsmen on the planet create this for him, utilising jewels from Zarkan's private treasure house. It was worth an emperor's ransom, but it had seemed like something he just had to have. After all, when you had an insect's head, you needed something that added a touch of class.

'Have you any idea where he went?' asked Skelp. 'The old emperor, I mean.'

'None whatsoever. But it's clear to me that the device that young boy wore was some kind of a booby trap, designed to eradicate anybody who touched it. I warned Emperor Zarkan not to press that button, but sadly he disregarded my advice.' Jinks lifted the crown and placed it carefully on his huge, domed head. He tilted it to a rakish angle, gave himself one last admiring look in the mirror and then turned to look at Skelp.

'So, what are we waiting for?' he cried. 'Let's get this show on the road!'

★ ★ ★

The sound of heavy boots clumping on stone alerted Kip to the fact that something was happening. He gazed around the cell at his companions – Mr Lazarus and Dario, Stephanie and Blutacca, all slumped on their benches, staring into space. Princess Shanna had been taken away days ago and they had seen neither hide nor hair of her since. As for the rest of them, it hadn't been the best three weeks they'd ever spent. They'd all been locked up in the cell with nothing to do and only occasional toilet breaks and several trays a day of revolting-looking food to break the monotony. Kip and Mr Lazarus feared that the excessive food wasn't a good sign, but Dario seemed happy enough to fatten himself up. He was actually getting used to a diet of grubs and insects and managed to finish off whatever the others left. Mr Lazarus now sported a grizzled white beard, while Dario had a thicker, black one. Stephanie's grey roots were starting to show and she spent most of her time in a complete grump, angry with Kip and with Mr Lazarus, for ever having invented a machine that could send people into movies. Only Blutacca remained the same, a big, hairy lump, sitting alone in one corner, glaring sullenly at the world with his tiny, teddy bear eyes.

Kip had mentioned several times to Mr Lazarus that they now had no hope of ever escaping from the film, since weeks had passed since their arrival, but Mr Lazarus kept assuring him that this would be compressed into just a couple of minutes in the film's running time and that they still had every chance of returning to real life. It was hard to know how such a thing might happen now. The Retriever was gone and there was no way of knowing where it might be.

The Draconians now approaching the cell were not the usual feeding detail – they were armed guards, one of them carrying a collection of heavy metal chains. Kip thought that he'd worked out the difference between them and the white suited space troopers. The Draconians got to do all the thankless donkey work. The space troopers were called in whenever a real fighting force was needed. The doors were opened and a couple of the guards entered the cell, holding a pulse rifle on the occupants whilst one Draconian cuffed them together, arm-to-arm, until they were all shackled in a line.

'What's all this in aid of?' growled Dario, but since none of the Draconians was wearing a translator, his words went unheeded. One of the lizard-men waved his pulse rifle and the five captives were ushered out of the cell in awkward, clanking single file and marched up the steps to the ground floor. They were escorted through the opulent palace chambers above and finally out into the terrace, the blaze of unfamiliar sunlight making them squint. Commander Skelp was waiting for them and Kip was relieved to see that he *was* wearing a translator.

'What's going on?' asked Mr Lazarus. 'Why have you brought us up here?'

Commander Skelp smiled mirthlessly. 'We didn't want you to miss any of the fun,' he croaked. 'Today is a special day.'

'Special in what way?' asked Kip nervously.

'Today our beloved emperor is marrying Princess Shanna,' said Skelp.

'Zarkan is marrying the princess?' cried Kip.

'Don't be coy with me, child!' sneered Skelp. 'As you know only too well, the Emperor Zarkan is missing, presumed dead.'

'He is?' muttered Mr Lazarus.

'Oh, don't pretend to be innocent,' Skelp warned him. 'We know it was all part of your cunning plan. But removing one emperor isn't going to change anything. I refer of course to our new emperor, the Emperor Jinks.'

'Jinks?' Stephanie looked appalled. 'That thing with the head of a giant greenfly? Princess Shanna is marrying *that*?' She pulled a face. 'Ugh! Well, rather her than me, that's for sure!'

'Your remark is impudent,' observed Skelp. 'In different circumstances, I would have you lashed. However, there's little point.'

'Come again?' said Kip.

'You are about to be taken to witness the wedding of Emperor Jinks and Princess Shanna,' explained Skelp. 'The emperor wanted to give you a last little treat before you are taken to the Coliseum.'

'Oh, we're going to the theatre?' said Dario, brightening. 'I *love* a good musical. What are we seeing?'

Skelp sniggered. 'A little show called *The Big Barbecue*,' he said.

'You mean, we're finally getting something decent to eat?' cried Dario. 'I can't believe it, we...' He broke off as the full meaning of Skelp's words sank in. 'Oh,' he said. 'Am I to take it we *are* the barbecue?'

'Correct,' said Skelp. He placed a hand tenderly, almost lovingly on Dario's shoulder. 'I'm really looking forward to it,' he said. 'I haven't eaten a human steak in ages.'

Dario groaned. 'Typical. The first decent food in weeks and I won't be getting any.'

'But...I can't be barbecued!' protested Stephanie. 'I...I work for the *Evening Post*!'

'My dear lady, I don't care if you work for the *Universal Express*, you're dead meat.'

'Just a minute,' said Kip. He was fighting his natural terror in an attempt to figure out what was going on. 'You told us the emperor Zarkan was missing. So...what exactly happened to him?'

'Stop pretending,' sneered Skelp. 'You know better than anyone! The Emperor touched that device you wore around your neck. One moment he was still with us, the next, he was gone.'

Kip and Mr Lazarus exchanged looks. 'But,' whispered Kip, 'that means....'

'That means what?' prompted Skelp suspiciously.

'Er...it means nothing,' said Mr Lazarus. He directed a warning look at Kip. 'Nothing at all.'

'Hmph! If I had my way, I'd torture the truth out of you. But when I suggested the idea to Jinks, he didn't seem keen.' Skelp shook his head. 'Well, time is moving on. And you lot have a wedding to get to. I'm afraid I can't accompany you, I have my duties as best man to consider. Oh yes, one last thing.' He walked along the line of chained figures, pressing a small paper bag into each of their hands.

'What's this?' muttered Dario.

'Confetti,' said Skelp. 'Make sure you save it until the happy couple are walking down the aisle. Now, on your way.' He snapped a command to the armed troops, who lifted their weapons and prodded at the captives to get them moving.

Kip looked at Mr Lazarus accusingly. He was just ahead of him in line. 'If the emperor's gone to the Paramount, what will have happened to Beth and Rose and the others?' he whispered.

'Oh, I'm sure they'll be fine,' said Mr Lazarus. 'Beth knows how to look after herself. And hopefully, they'll have the sense to send him straight back again. I know he seems to have been gone for weeks, but it might just be minutes to him.'

'You think so?'

'There's every chance. And maybe . . . just maybe, he'll still have the Retriever with him. If we can just get hold of it, we might still have a fighting chance of getting home.'

The nearest Draconian barked a command and they were marched across the great stone plaza through the milling crowds of alien creatures. But for the first time in ages, Kip felt a sense of hope stirring within him.

CHAPTER TWENTY-THREE

The Reluctant Bride

Princess Shanna was feeling particularly odd this morning. She had a slow, floaty feeling in her head. She told herself that today was the day she was going to be made to marry a man with an oversized insect's head and that she really ought to be furious, but somehow she just couldn't bring herself to get worked up about it.

She examined her reflection in the full-length mirror. The white lace and silk wedding dress was the kind of thing that every self-respecting princess dreamed of wearing one day. But her childhood fantasies had always revolved around a handsome young prince, not something that looked like it ought to be struck repeatedly with a rolled-up newspaper. She told herself that she really should be thinking up a plan of escape, but this morning her brain seemed incapable of working out anything more difficult than which shoes to wear.

The door to her chamber opened and Jinks

poked his hideous head into the room, his antennae twitching. 'Ah, Princess!' he said. 'I know it's supposed to be bad luck, but I somehow couldn't resist dropping by to get a look at you in that outfit.' He stepped into the room and studied her appreciatively. 'I have to say you look good enough to eat. Er . . . not that I'd ever *do* that, of course, it's just an expression.' He gestured at the dress. 'Do you like it?' he asked eagerly. 'I scoured the galaxy for the hottest new designer and finally found what I was looking for on Morpheus Twelve. The lady who designed that frock is the biggest name in the Universe. And not just because she's called Jumbelaria Attafrangen Frunterbunk!'

'Is that right?' Princess Shanna stood there, swaying slightly as she gazed at her husband-to-be. The thought of walking down the aisle with him should be reducing her to a screaming fit, but she just felt it would be too much effort. 'How . . . how long do I have?' she mumbled. 'Before the . . . wedding?'

'Not long, sweetness. The Imperial carriage will be arriving out front in ten clicks. As custom dictates, I'll be going on ahead of you. Oh, Princess, I can't wait until we're insectoid and wife! See you later!' He went out, closing the door behind him

272

and Princess Shanna was left alone in the big empty room, gazing at the mirror and, through the woozy fog in her head, a thought occurred. Where the heck was Zeke? Was he even still alive? And if he was, why hadn't he come to rescue her?

★ ★ ★

In the projection room, Beth was still trying to pick her moment. When she'd first looked through the hatch, she'd caught the tail end of a scene featuring Jinks standing in front of a mirror, and she'd thought she could give the emperor the face-to-face he'd requested, but just as she was readying herself to tell Rose to push the platform forward into the light, the scene had cut to one featuring Princess Shanna in almost exactly the same pose, and she'd told the emperor to hang on a bit, be patient.

She'd lost concentration for a moment, which was bad, because no sooner had she taken her eyes off the screen, than Jinks popped his head into the next scene, catching Beth off guard. She'd readied herself for a second attempt, but Jinks was in that scene so briefly, she'd had to abandon the move again.

'Come along, girl,' hissed the emperor. 'What's the problem?'

'It's not as easy as it looks,' Beth assured him. 'Is it, Rose?'

'No, we have to get this just right,' Rose told him, her foot still poised on the wooden platform. 'You want to end up next to the insect-headed man, right?'

'Yes, but—'

'So stop talking and let us concentrate! If we get it wrong you could end up on another planet or just floating around in space. You wouldn't want that, would you?'

The emperor muttered something under his breath.

Beth studied the screen. Now there was a long shot of a huge, white church-like building, the camera tracking closer to it. She could see people hurrying across a square towards it, as bells rang out, announcing a joyful occasion. She caught a brief glimpse of some chained figures walking in single file through the midst of the crowd and thought that one of them might be Kip, but the camera swooped onwards and she couldn't be sure.

'What's going on now?' asked the emperor, impatiently.

'Dunno. Looks like a wedding or something...'

'That will be Jinks's marriage to Princess Shanna,' said the emperor, through gritted teeth.

'Did I miss something?' asked Beth, puzzled.

'Yes, while you were frozen,' said Rose. 'Jinks is the new emperor and he's getting married to Princess Shanna.'

'No way!' said Beth.

'Way!' said Rose.

'If I don't get to him soon,' snarled the emperor, 'it'll be too late.'

'Yes, yes,' said Rose. 'Give us a minute!'

'Look, forget about the face-to-face,' urged the emperor. 'Just put me into the city square, I'll make my own way into the cathedral.'

Rose glared at him. 'Just give us time to...'

'NOW!' roared the emperor.

'Oh, have it your own way!' Rose gave up and thrust one foot hard against the wooden platform. It slid forward into the light and the emperor's cloaked figure shimmered for a moment, then vanished. Rose let out a long breath and turned to look at Beth, who was standing at the viewing window, an expression of surprise on her face. 'Honestly,' said Rose. 'Those flipping evil emperors. They can't be bothered to wait for *anything.*'

★ ★ ★

Kip made his way across the crowded square, flanked by armed Draconian troops. He was handcuffed to Mr Lazarus, who was handcuffed to Dario, who was handcuffed to Stephanie, who was handcuffed to Blutacca. They moved along in a shambling, swaying line, blinking in the unaccustomed sunlight, uncomfortably aware that every creature they passed was looking at them in an expectant way. Some of them were actually licking their lips.

'I suppose the wedding must be taking place there,' said Kip, nodding his head towards the huge building on the far side of the square.

'Yes, and after that, we're all going to be cooked and eaten,' said Dario bleakly. 'In public.'

'Thanks for the reminder,' said Kip glumly.

'It won't come to that,' said Mr Lazarus, clearly trying to stay positive. In the daylight, Kip could see that he was now well on the way to acquiring a full grey beard. 'You'll see, something will come up. It always does.'

'They needn't think they're going to try any of that funny business with me,' said Stephanie, from further up the line. 'If they barbecue me, I'll write a letter of complaint they'll never forget.'

'I fail to see how you'll write anything if you've been eaten,' said Dario.

'Groogle thwange ronkle punt,' said Blutacca, which probably meant something like, 'Stop bickering, you two.'

Now Kip could see that he'd been right about the venue. He couldn't help feeling that this time he was in a fix he couldn't get out of. It prompted him to speak aloud.

'Beth, I don't know if you can hear me right now,' he said. 'But just in case you can, I have to tell you that things aren't looking good here. If anything bad happens to me, and I don't manage to make it back, I want you to know... that you can have my collection of film posters, action figures and DVDs.'

Mr Lazarus looked at him. 'It's going to be all right,' he said.

'You don't know that,' said Kip. 'You're just hoping for the best.'

'When all else fails,' said Mr Lazarus, 'I find that's the only course of action.'

The troopers were herding them in the direction of a huge, gleaming churchlike building, the spires of which rose to dizzy heights against the purple sky. The noise of ringing bells was getting rapidly louder.

'These creatures have a *religion*?' muttered Dario in disbelief. 'Who'd have thought it?'

'Most races have some kind of religion,' observed Mr Lazarus. 'They probably worship a lizard-god.'

'Godzilla,' muttered Dario. 'Or maybe the Lizard of Oz.'

Now they were being shepherded up the long flight of white stone steps to the entrance. They went in through the massive open doors and found themselves in what could only be described as a nave. Rows of wooden benches lay on either side of them and, at the top of a straight central aisle, there was some kind of stone altar dominated by a huge painting of a cloaked and hooded figure.

'The Emperor,' observed Mr Lazarus. 'So that's who they worship round here.'

'Yes, but which one?' asked Kip. 'You can't even see the face. It could be anyone.'

'Most likely it's whoever inherits the cloak,' said Mr Lazarus.

Kip and his companions were marched straight along the aisle and then made to sit down on the floor, a short distance from the altar. Behind them, the wooden benches began to fill up with worshippers, mostly lizard-men and women, but there were other weird creatures dotted amongst them. Kip noticed one beast that had a head like a blob of pulsating jelly and a couple of others that had faces like fish.

'Odd-looking bunch,' observed Dario – and instantly one of the guards hissed something at him that was clearly an instruction to shut his mouth. 'All right,' he said, 'there's no need to be touchy.'

Soon the wooden benches were full and there was a mounting sense of expectation in the air. A squid-like creature shambled over to some kind of wooden harp, and a series of tentacles, sprouting from his sides began to meander over the strings, coaxing forth a loud and discordant jangling that was doubtless intended to be music. Then, sensing a movement behind him, Kip glanced over his shoulder and saw Jambo Jinks and Commander Skelp walking slowly up the aisle, dressed in their finest uniforms.

'Here comes the groom,' said Mr Lazarus. 'I expect Princess Shanna will be along in a few minutes.'

'She *can't* marry Jinks,' hissed Kip. 'She's already engaged to Zeke.'

'I doubt Jinks is bothered about that little detail,' said Mr Lazarus.

'If she's a married woman then Zeke will have to look elsewhere,' said Stephanie hopefully, and everybody looked at her pityingly.

They fell silent as Jinks and Skelp walked past them. Skelp moved off to one side and Jinks turned back to survey the rows of seated people. A Draconian soldier brought forward some kind of microphone on a stand and placed it in front of him. Kip noticed that the device was flashing with a whole series of coloured lights and surmised that it must be some kind of multi-translator, which would simultaneously translate Jinks's words into the languages of all the different races present. 'Citizens of Volpin Eight,' he said, his voice ringing out loud and clear across the vast room. 'I thank you for coming here today to witness my marriage to the Princess Shanna.'

'Not all of us had a choice,' muttered Dario, then piped down as one of the Draconians threatened to slam a rifle butt into his side. Jinks looked sternly down at the captives for a moment, before continuing. 'As you can see, I have brought before you the enemies of our planet – the captive Earthlings who plotted to assassinate our beloved emperor and who actually caused his disappearance.'

This remark coaxed a lot of mumbling and muttering from the benches. A sea of faces turned to look at Kip and the others, and Kip squirmed uncomfortably. What could he do?

'You will be glad to know that, directly after this joyful occasion, all of these evil creatures will be dragged in chains to the arena where there will be a free barbecue for every citizen of Volpin Eight. And as a special thank you from myself and my bride there will be an extra bank holiday this year!'

At this, a cheer went up. Kip looked desperately at Mr Lazarus.

'This is starting to look bad,' he hissed. 'We're going to be eaten. There's no way out.'

'Don't worry,' the old man told him. 'This is a movie. It can't end like this. Something is bound to turn up.'

'I hope you're right,' said Kip grimly. 'I really do.'

Jinks raised his hands to quell the noise. 'And so,

my loyal subjects, the time is at hand. Bring on the high priest! Bring out the bride! Let's get this party started!'

CHAPTER TWENTY-FOUR

Weddings R Us

The awful, ear-melting music began again and from behind the altar a high priest appeared – a Draconian dressed in a glittering golden cloak and a strange pointed hat, decorated with images of planets and spaceships. He came to stand in front of Jinks and Skelp, a heavy leather-bound book clutched in his scaly hands. Jinks turned to look down the aisle and Kip followed his gaze. He saw Princess Shanna coming towards the altar, swaying and lurching in an extraordinary fashion, as though she'd stopped at several bars on her way here. She was wearing a dress of white silk and lace, with a long, flowing train stretching out behind her and she was clutching a large bunch of multicoloured orchid-like flowers. She looked beautiful but Kip was immediately worried for her, because she didn't seem too bothered about being forced to marry a man with the head of a cockroach. She was gazing around with a big dopey smile on her face, as though she hadn't quite worked out what she was doing here but had decided to make the best of it anyway.

As she passed by Kip and the others, she threw a puzzled smile in their direction and said, 'Oh, hi, guys! I wondered what had happened to you. Lovely day for it, huh?' Then she strolled merrily on to meet Jinks.

'What's up with her?' hissed Kip. He had no idea why the princess wasn't trying to fight this.

'I'd say she's drunk,' muttered Dario.

'Or drugged,' suggested Mr Lazarus.

'She'd need to be,' said Stephanie. 'Have you seen the state of the groom? What a minger! I tell you what, I wouldn't fancy it.'

This remark prompted another hissing screech from the nearest Draconian guard.

'Yes, all right!' said Dario. 'We get the general idea!'

Jinks stepped forward and took the princess's hand in his. 'You look captivating,' he told Princess Shanna.

She gazed back at him. 'And you look... really weird,' she said. 'Nobody told me it was fancy dress!'

Jinks snickered obligingly and then turned back to face the high priest. 'Let's do this thing,' he said.

The priest bowed his head. 'Oh course, your Majesty.' He opened the heavy book and then swept a stern gaze over the assembled congregation. When he spoke, his amplified words echoed under the domed roof. 'People of Volpin Eight,' he croaked. 'We are gathered here today for the wedding of his Majesty, the Supreme Emperor Jambo Excelsior Colin Jinks and her Majesty, the Princess Shanna Veronica Thornaby of the planet Enterrium Two in the constellation of Auximines, in the sure and certain knowledge that their union is one that has been decreed by destiny itself. Before I proceed, according to the great traditions of our planet, I ask that if anyone here knows of any just cause or impediment to this union, speak now or for ever hold your peace.'

There was a long silence and the priest was about to continue when a hoarse and strangely familiar voice from somewhere at the back of the cathedral interrupted him. Kip experienced a sudden rush of fresh hope.

'I can think of a very good impediment,' it said.

Jinks span round, his antennae twitching. 'Who

said that?' he shrieked. 'How dare somebody interrupt the solemnity of this occasion with such a flippant remark? Guards, seize that fool and have him ejected from the building!'

But none of the guards made a move towards the figure that had just appeared at the top of the aisle – a cloaked and hooded figure that was now gliding slowly towards the altar, speaking as it came. 'The problem is, for there to be a new emperor the old one would have to have died . . . but as you can see, I am still very much alive.'

Jinks's huge eyes bulged. He stood there, as though transfixed, his mouthparts moving but making no sound.

Zarkan kept coming and, as he moved closer, Kip noticed a really important detail. Something was dangling from one of his hands by a length of chain. The Retriever! He jabbed an elbow into Mr Lazarus's ribs and pointed.

'I see it!' hissed Mr Lazarus.

Hope rose up in Kip's heart. He'd never thought that he'd be pleased to see the evil emperor, but his sudden arrival meant that maybe Kip and his friends still had a chance! He watched intently as the scene unfolded.

The emperor kept talking in that hoarse, chilling whisper. 'The other thing is that for Jinks to be proclaimed emperor in my place, it would necessitate me naming him as my successor. Something that I never actually *did*.'

This caused a sharp intake of breath from the assembled congregation.

Jinks finally found his voice and started blabbering. 'Your... Your Majesty! What a relief to find you alive and well! You've no idea how worried we've all been. I've lain awake every night wondering what might have become of you. Thank goodness that fate has seen fit to return you to your—'

'Cease your prattle,' said the emperor sternly and Jinks fell silent. Zarkan stopped a short distance from Jinks and turned to look around at the congregation. 'So,' he said, 'it's your wedding day, Jinks. How delightful! And how nice to see so many fine citizens have come here to support you. If I'd known, I'd have brought you a present myself.' He turned back. 'And you think yourself a worthy husband for the princess, do you?'

'Er... well, Your Majesty, I thought it a... good match and er... a useful basis for peace between our planet and that of Enterrium Two, which I understand is rich in minerals and other useful products. Of course, if I'd been aware that there was any chance of your returning, I would never have...'

'And how, may I enquire, were you named as my successor?'

'Er...well, Your Majesty, we...we found your will and...'

'My will? That's very curious, considering I never left one.'

There was another incredulous gasp from the crowd. Kip scanned the room, trying to work out how he could get his hands on the Retriever but, for the moment, shackled as he was, he couldn't see a way of reaching it.

'Hey, Zarkan, baby, how are you doing?' Princess Shanna asked loudly, and every eye in the room turned to look at her. 'I mean, it's cool you could come and everything, dude, but this is a wedding, you really need to lighten up.'

'Is that a fact?' hissed the emperor.

'Oh, yeah, seriously. I love the cloak, by the way. Totally cool.'

'Why thank you, Your Majesty,' said the emperor, bowing his head. 'Just a little thing I threw on.

But if you'll forgive me, I'd like to hear Jinks's explanation.'

'Oh sure, be my guest.'

'But . . . we . . . we *did* find a will, your Majesty. Written in your own distinctive handwriting. I . . . I can't imagine how it could have come to be there, if you didn't actually write it.' Jinks looked accusingly at the captives in front of him. 'These earthlings must have done it!' he cried. 'Yes, that's it! Another part of their fiendish plan to overthrow you!'

'Hmm.' The Emperor lifted a hand to his head as though deep in thought. 'I'm not convinced,' he said. 'I fail to see a motive for them to have done such a thing. On the other hand, could it be, Jinks, that after all the documents you've signed on my behalf, you have learned to do a fair approximation of my handwriting? Could it be that *you* decided to forge the will and name yourself as my successor?'

There was a long, uncomfortable silence. 'I, my Lord? Forge the will? Surely you can't believe that I would stoop so low as to—'

'Jinks.' The emperor lifted a fist and pointed it at Jinks's chest. 'After some consideration, I have only one thing left to say to you.'

'Really, your Majesty? And...what is that, exactly?'

'You're fired.' With that a burst of white light shot out of the emperor's signet ring and hit Jinks full in the chest. It was clearly a more powerful weapon than his purple freezing ray. It lifted Jinks clean off his feet and blasted him backwards, knocking the hat off the high priest and punching the insect's flailing body clean through the portrait on the altar and back towards the rear wall of the cathedral. His priceless crown, knocked from his head by the impact, rolled onto the ground a metre or so from the chained captives.

A shocked silence descended. Then Princess Shanna said, 'Wow, far out! That was, like, a really neat trick.'

'Thank you, your Majesty,' said the emperor. He turned back to face the shocked crowd and bowed once again. 'My apologies for the delay, ladies and gentlemen. Since Senator Jinks appears to be indisposed and, not wanting to spoil this special occasion, I shall marry the Princess in his place. The Rebel Alliance will then be powerless to resist me...and Stardancer will be incredibly miffed.' He gave a low, throaty chuckle and turned back to

290

the author, reached out a wizened hand and took hold of Princess Shanna's arm. Then he gestured to the rather stunned and hatless high priest. 'You may continue,' he told him.

'Er . . . y . . . yes, Your Majesty,' stammered the high priest.

'Hey, hold on a moment!' protested Princess Shanna. 'Time out! I was just getting used to the idea of marrying Mr Cockroach back there. I don't want to seem rude, but like, how old are you?'

The emperor turned to gaze at her. 'In the manner in which time is measured on your home planet, I would say about one thousand and sixty years,' he told her. 'Give or take a few months.'

'Whoah! I've heard of marrying a more mature man, but that's pushing things,' said the princess. 'You're so mature, you're going off!' She turned to look down at the captives huddled in front of her. 'Are you guys just gonna sit there and let him get away with this?'

There was another long silence during which Kip wondered how close he was to the guard holding the keys to their handcuffs. He was just looking around for something to crack him over the head with, when suddenly he realised that the silence had been broken by a distant sound – the roaring of a jet engine. It was little more than a murmur at first, but it grew louder by the second. The emperor stepped away from the princess and stood there, looking in all directions. The Draconian guards shouldered their weapons. Now Kip heard the zapping of pulse rifles and a muffled explosion off across the square. Through the huge stained-glass window set high into the back wall of the cathedral, he saw a dark shape – a shape that was growing rapidly larger as it raced towards the glass. He braced himself for the impact.

Then there was an ear-splitting crash as something burst through the window, shattering the glass into a zillion pieces – and Kip saw to his amazement that it was Zeke, sitting astride some kind of a jet bike. He was hunched low over the controls, and in one hand he held a laser pistol. The bike skewed sideways for a moment, its engine faltering. Then it corrected itself and came racing low over the altar, heading straight towards the emperor, smashing what was left of the already ruined portrait to smithereens. The emperor saw the bike coming and turned to run. Kip saw the emperor drop the Retriever and accidentally step on Jinks's crown, lose his footing and fall over a bench to disappear behind a jumble of wooden furniture.

Then the bike was soaring onwards, over the heads of the screaming, panicking congregation. 'Get him!' yelled Skelp, running forward to join the guards assigned to watch over the captives. They turned, raising their weapons to fire at the jet bike, and Blutacca took the opportunity to leap to his feet and bring a heavy fist down onto the head of the nearest guard, stopping the man in his tracks. Kip noticed a big bunch of keys dangling from the guard's belt and he scrambled forward to make a grab at them. He pulled them free and started trying to locate the key that unlocked the cuffs.

'Yes,' whispered Mr Lazarus. 'Good boy, that's the ticket!'

'Undo me first,' added Dario.

There was a squawk from just behind him and a figure pitched backwards over Kip's head, smoke billowing from a hole in his breastplate. It was Commander Skelp and it was evident at a glance that he wasn't going to be causing any more trouble. Kip looked frantically over his shoulder and saw that Zeke had banked low over the heads of the crowd, who were now pushing and shoving their way towards the exit. He was coming back, firing a pulse pistol as he came, blasting guards off their feet with deadly accuracy. Kip redoubled his efforts, finally located the right key and unlocked his cuff. He handed the key to Mr Lazarus, then looked around desperately and finally saw the Retriever lying on the tiled floor only a short distance away. He scrambled to his feet and made a beeline for it. But just as he reached out a hand to pick it up, a guard ran by him and caught it a glancing blow with his foot, sending it skittering across the tiled floor.

'No!' Kip cursed and went after it, telling himself he had to get hold of it at all costs. Another guard made a grab for him and he swerved sideways, tripping the man and sending him sprawling. Time was running out and Kip knew it. This had to be the last big action set piece of the film. He saw the Retriever go spinning under a wooden pew and he threw himself face down on the floor and went sliding after it, one arm extended. *Argh!* The gap was too small for his hand to go under. He lay there, wondering what to do, and then something rolled across the floor and came to a rest right beside him. A laser sword! He snatched it up, jumped to his feet and pressed the button. A beam of blue light shot into the air. Kip swung the weapon overhead and, with a flashing of sparks, the heavy wooden bench parted like soft cheese under a knife. Kip hit the button again, stuffed the laser sword into his belt and kicked the bench aside, revealing the Retriever. He stooped, snatched it up with a cry of delight. As he did so he saw Zeke's jet bike swoop down alongside the princess. Zeke flung his empty pistol aside.

'Hi, honey,' he said.

'What time do you call this?' she asked him – as though the mere sight of her saviour was enough to snap her out of her drugged haze. He ignored the question, threw a powerful arm around her waist and lifted her onto the seat behind him, then snatched a moment to kiss her, in the best action-hero tradition. He turned to look at the captives, who were now free of their chains and up on their feet. 'Room for one more!' he bellowed and beckoned frantically. Blutacca gave a bellow of delight and ran to the jet bike, but unfortunately, so did Stephanie. They both reached it at the same time and stood there, staring at each other in dull surprise.

Zeke looked from one to the other, seemingly undecided. Then he frowned, shook his head. 'I'm sorry, Stephanie,' he said. 'You're really great and everything and in different circumstances we could have been good together. But a man can never really escape his destiny. And besides . . . me and Blooey go back a long way.' He nodded to Blutacca and the Silonian climbed onto the rear pillion.

'But, Zeke!' cried Stephanie. 'What about me?'

'What about you?' muttered Princess Shanna. 'Where did you get that dress, honey, the Silonian thrift store?

Zeke looked troubled. 'Stephanie,' he murmured. 'I'm afraid you're . . .'

' . . . history,' said a croaking voice. Kip turned in surprise to see that the emperor was getting back to his feet, emerging from behind a pile of scattered wooden benches. His hood had slipped back from his head, revealing a hideous, toothless face that was a bloodless misery of wizened, twisted lines. He looked every single one of his thousand and sixty years. 'So, Stardancer,' he whispered, 'our game finally concludes. Perhaps before you die, you'll tell me why you have pursued me so relentlessly over the years.' He was lifting his clenched fist, aiming the power ring to blast the three figures on the jet bike out of existence.

'You killed my parents!' yelled Zeke.

There was a silence. 'Oh, *that*,' said the emperor. 'Well, your father was a bit of a twit, you know. Always moaning about every little thing. And your mother was a really terrible cook, as I recall. So no great loss to anyone, really.' He clenched his fist tighter. 'Goodbye, Zeke,' he said. 'I'm going to miss you.'

Kip acted instinctively. He ran across the intervening space and launched himself feet first at the emperor, his trainers slamming into Zarkan's chest and sending him flailing backwards with a grunt of surprise, his right arm still extended. The signet ring flashed, sending a ray of pure white fire blazing upwards to the ceiling as he fell. He landed heavily amongst the litter of furniture.

'Oww,' he said. 'You little git, that really hurt.' He started to get up again, intent on revenge, and Kip reached instinctively for the laser sword. But then there was a grinding roar from above and clouds of dust began to sift down from the shattered ceiling. 'Oh, poo,' said the emperor, staring upwards. Then a huge slab of masonry broke away and fell onto him, crushing him flat. A great cloud of plaster dust billowed down from a gaping hole in the ceiling.

Kip got back to his feet and gazed open-mouthed at the destruction he'd inadvertently caused. 'Sorry,' he said. He turned to look towards the jet bike.

Zeke stared back at him in amazement and grinned his film star grin. 'Thanks, young traveller,' he said. 'I am indebted to you. And I'm glad you found your friends.' Blutacca gave his a thumbs-up. 'Yowza!' he barked. Zeke gestured at the heavily laden bike. 'I don't have any more room. Once I've taken these two to safety, I'll return for you all, my friends.'

'No need.' Kip assured him. He lifted the Retriever. 'I can get the rest of us home with this.' The sound of running feet alerted Kip to the fact that a detachment of space troopers were coming in through the entrance, trying to find their way through the thick fog of dust. 'Better get moving,' he warned Zeke.

Zeke nodded. He slammed the jet bike into gear, levitated it to a safe height and then soared forward, heading straight for the already smashed window at the back of the cathedral. The passengers ducked their heads at the last instant and then they were gone, zooming out into the wild blue yonder. Kip heard Blutacca yell a last, triumphant, 'Yabba Rabba Flunge!'

'Zeke!' cried Stephanie, tears filling her eyes behind the thick lenses of her glasses. 'Come back! I love you!'

'There's no time for that rubbish,' Kip told her. He grabbed her arm and dragged her across the room towards Mr Lazarus and Dario. This had to be the final scene of the movie. 'Everybody hold on to me!' he yelled. 'Time we were out of here.' But even as Kip ran to Mr Lazarus, he realised that Dario had detached himself from his brother and moved away, his attention caught by something bright and glittery lying on the floor just a few steps away. Jinks's crown.

'No, Dario, leave it!' yelled Mr Lazarus. 'We have to go NOW!' Just at that moment, Kip and Stephanie reached him and wrapped their arms around him.

Kip flipped the cover off the eject button. 'Come on!'

'Just hang on a moment,' shouted Dario. 'This thing must be worth a fortune.'

'Dario, there isn't time!' roared Mr Lazarus.

Dario ignored him. He bent over and snatched up the crown, then straightened up and held it aloft, with a cry of triumph. 'Got it!' he bellowed. 'At last, I'm a rich man!'

And then two burley space troopers came running out of the dust cloud and wrestled him to the ground.

'Dario!' screamed Mr Lazarus, and he tried to break out of the huddle – but Kip clung onto him, knowing they dare not delay any longer. He was aware of armed troopers emerging from the dust cloud, their weapons raised to fire. He pressed the eject button. For a long moment nothing happened, and he feared he'd left it too late. But then he felt the melting sensation deep inside him and he and the others were falling into a brilliant white light.

Something beneath them lurched suddenly backwards and they fell off the wooden platform in an untidy sprawl. Kip blinked and looked up to see the familiar surroundings of the projection room and Beth and Rose gazing down at him, looks of sheer relief on their faces.

Then Beth lunged at him and threw her arms

around his neck, hugging him close. 'Oh, Kip,' she cried. 'That was so close. I thought I'd lost you for ever!'

'Smile,' said Rose. As they turned to look at her, she lifted her mobile and snapped a picture.

Epilogue

For a moment, everything seemed frozen in time. Then Kip managed to detach himself from Beth's arms and he looked around the room. He could see that all three of them had made it back safely but it was clear from Mr Lazarus's grim expression that he was distraught about leaving his brother behind. He must have known, from bitter experience, that there was absolutely nothing that could be done about the situation now. From the auditorium, they could hear that famous theme tune playing over the closing credits.

Kip went to Mr Lazarus and put a hand on his shoulder. 'I'm really sorry about Dario,' he muttered. 'But if I hadn't pressed the button when I did . . .'

Mr Lazarus nodded. 'I know,' he said. 'I don't blame you, Kip. Not for one moment. And Dario should have left the crown well alone. I always said that greedy streak would get him into trouble one day.'

'Maybe you'll be able to go back for him another time,' said Beth, but they all knew that wasn't possible. If you were still in the movie when the credits rolled, you were stuck there for ever – those were the rules of the Lazarus Enigma.

'Poor Dario,' muttered Mr Lazarus. 'To think he'll spend the rest of his days eating bugs and being sick. He isn't going to enjoy that at all.'

Kip remembered something. He reached down to his belt and pulled out the laser sword. He handed it to Mr Lazarus. 'I know it doesn't make up for losing your brother,' he said. 'But it's what you wanted, right?'

The old man nodded and sighed. Kip smiled encouragingly, then lifted his head and looked at Beth. 'What's the situation here?'

'Not good,' she told him. 'We've got a cinema full of frozen people out there. They'll be snapping out of it any time now and when they do... well, they'll know everything.'

'That's terrible.' Kip thought for a moment. 'Mr L, can you do anything?'

Mr Lazarus nodded and seemed to make an effort to shake off his sorrow. 'We'll have to act quickly.' He looked at the others. 'You must all stay here with the doors closed. If you think there's any danger of overhearing what I say out there, put your fingers in your ears . . . unless, of course, you want to forget everything that's happened here tonight.'

'I don't get it,' said Kip. 'What are you going to . . . ?' Then he remembered how Mr Lazarus had hypnotised Rose to make her 'forget' about *Terror Island*. 'Will it work with so many people?' he asked.

'I think so. As long as they can hear what I'm saying as they're waking up.' He glanced at Rose. 'Maybe you would like to come with me and join in with the others?' he suggested.

'No way,' said Rose. 'I want to remember it this time.'

'You understand that it has to be a secret?' Kip asked her anxiously.

She nodded. 'Don't worry,' she told him. And she reached up a finger and thumb and pulled them across her mouth, to indicate that her lips were sealed.

'Very well, my dear,' said Mr Lazarus. He glanced uncertainly at Stephanie. 'As for you, Miss Holder, I'm also going to have to ask you to keep our little secret. I know it must go against the grain for somebody in your profession, but . . .'

'Who'd believe it, anyway?' asked Stephanie glumly. 'If I started telling people that Zeke Stardancer had the hots for me, they'd think I was stark staring bonkers.' She looked at Beth and Rose. 'He did though, didn't he? Until that flipping princess turned up. You must have seen how he acted around me?'

'Er...' Beth shrugged her shoulders. 'Yeah, he *did* seem a bit keen, Stephanie, but... well, I've seen this before. In the end, those movie people always go with the script.'

'I don't know why,' said Stephanie. 'That Princess Shanna... what's she got that I haven't?'

There was a long, uncomfortable silence. Nobody seemed to have an answer for that.

'I'd better get out there,' said Mr Lazarus. 'The audience could be waking up at any moment.' He set the laser sword down on his work bench. 'Also, Kip, we're going to need to order up another print of the film for tomorrow night. Tell them it's an emergency. We can't allow anybody else to see this one. We'll have to tell them we had an accident with it.' He nodded to the spool of film that was still running through the projector as the seemingly endless credits played. Kip knew that now there would be one extra credit amongst the actors. Dario Lazarus as *Fat Earthling*, or something similar. 'That spool will have to go in my special collection,' said Mr Lazarus. 'Don't worry, I'll handle any costs incurred. There's no need to trouble your father with this.'

Kip nodded and then frowned. 'Where *is* Dad?' he asked.

'He's frozen halfway up the stairs,' said Rose matter-of-factly. 'He was being chased by people who wanted their money back.'

Kip grimaced and glanced at Mr Lazarus. 'This had better work,' he said, 'or we've all got some explaining to do.'

'Leave it to me,' said Mr Lazarus. He went quickly out of the room, closing the door behind him. Kip went to the projection window and saw the old man making his way down the crowded stairs, moving in and out of the frozen figures, one of whom was Dad. The old man took up his position in front of the screen, pulled an ancient watch from his waistcoat pocket and held it up in front of him, dangling on a length of chain. Kip knew he was waiting for that moment when everybody began to wake up. He also knew pretty much what he was going to say. 'Ladies and gentlemen, may I have your attention please? I have something very important to tell you. Concentrate on the watch. You are becoming very, very sleepy... and you will forget everything that has happened here tonight...'

Kip sighed. He turned back to the others. 'Poor Mr L,' he said. 'He must be really upset about his brother.'

Beth shook her head. 'If you ask me, it's a good thing,' she said. Everyone looked at her. 'I know it sounds mean, but think about it for a moment. Dario was causing big trouble... Mr L was even talking about leaving the Paramount. And don't forget, it was Dario's fault he even ended up in *Space Blasters* in the first place. With his brother stuck in that copy of the film, life is going to be so much easier for everyone. And he was a hundred and seventeen years old.'

'I suppose,' agreed Kip. 'But it does seem a bit harsh.' He looked down at Stephanie, who was sitting on the floor, her chin in her hands. 'Honestly, you're better off this way,' he told her. 'If Zeke had taken you with him you'd have been stuck there, doing the same stupid things over and over again.'

'I suppose. But I'd have been doing them with Zeke Skydancer, wouldn't I? Instead of which, I'm back to a dead end job on a dead end newspaper.' She sighed. 'All in all, this has been a complete disaster. I won't be able to file a story for the paper. I even lost the camera and they asked me to use it to get a snap of the Special Guest Star.'

Rose stepped forward, holding out her mobile phone. 'I think I can help with that,' she said.

Kip made a sound of irritation. 'She can't use a photograph of me and Beth hugging,' he told her. 'Who wants to see that?'

'That's not what I meant,' said Rose. She clicked a button and displayed a picture. Everyone stared at it in amazement. It showed the Emperor Zarkan, standing in front of the screen at the Paramount, his arms spread wide. Behind him, on the screen, there was a huge close-up of Jambo Jinks, his bug eyes staring out at the audience.

'Wow,' said Kip. He looked at Beth. 'I'd forgotten the emperor came here! He . . . he didn't hurt you or anything, did he?

'Don't worry,' Rose assured him. 'We handled him, no problem.'

'Slice of fish,' said Beth with a wink.

Stephanie was still looking at the photograph. 'Now *that*,' she said, 'is what I call a Special Guest Star!'

★ ★ ★

Mr McCall came back to his senses and found that he was standing halfway up the stairs of the Paramount Picture Palace. A familiar voice from behind him appeared to be talking, telling him that he had some important information . . .

He turned and his head seemed to swim for a moment and when his senses returned for the second time, he found he was standing in the midst of a whole load of people, most of whom were in the act of leaving the cinema. He blinked, trying to understand what had just happened to him. How did he even get here? The last thing he remembered was posing for a photograph with some space troopers at the entrance to the Paramount, but what had happened since then? He couldn't for the life of him remember. But he told himself, the event must have been a success. The cinema looked packed to bursting point.

He noticed that a crowd was gathering by the

exit doors, so he pushed his way through until he was out in the foyer and then he saw that people were unable to leave, because the main doors were locked. But he didn't remember locking them. Apologising profusely, he managed to struggle through the pushing, shoving people, fumbling for the keys as he went. He got to the door and noticed a hastily scrawled HOUSE FULL sign taped to it. Something else he didn't remember doing. He unlocked the door and pushed it open, then turned back to say goodbye to the audience as they went by him. They all looked blankly at him as they stumbled past, as though they had recently awoken from a deep sleep. Surely the film couldn't have been as boring as that? Even the little kids looked blank-eyed and sleepy. Dad spotted Norman and Kitty coming towards him and waved at them. Norman was a film buff and always had lots to say about each new release. 'Hi, Norman,' said Dad. 'What did you think of the film?'

Norman gave him an odd look. 'Yes,' he said, 'it was, er...umm...' He shook his head. 'It's the oddest thing, but I can't seem to remember anything about it.' He looked at Kitty. 'What did you think?'

She had the same vacant expression. 'I seem to remember it was . . . something to do with outer space,' she said unhelpfully. 'Wasn't it?'

'Er . . . right,' said Dad. 'Well . . . thanks for that. Nice to see you both. Do come again.'

They smiled and moved past him into the street, followed by more and more people, all shuffling into the night like a troop of brainwashed zombies. The two space troopers went clanking by, their rifles over their shoulders, but when Dad asked if they'd enjoyed the film, he got nothing more than grunts in reply. He waited until the last few stragglers were gone, then went back inside and locked the door behind him. A glance at the cashbox in the office reassured him that everything had indeed gone very well. It was liberally stuffed with banknotes.

He locked the money in the safe for the night, then left the office and made his way through into the auditorium to find his children, who were with Beth, Mr Lazarus and the journalist from the *Evening Post,* sitting in the seats at the front, gazing thoughtfully up at the screen.

'Looks like we did really well tonight,' Kip's dad said as he joined them.

'Yeah, it was great, wasn't it?' said Kip, a little too loudly. He was suddenly very aware of his filthy clothes, and the fact that his hair was much longer and greasier than the last time he'd seen his father.

'I'd say it was the best film yet,' said Mr Lazarus. 'Though it had a very sad ending.' Kip noticed how Dad's mouth dropped open at the sight of his projectionist, who despite being clean-shaven for that photograph outside the cinema, was now sporting a white beard. 'I particularly liked the way the young hero risked everything to save his old friend,' added Mr Lazarus. 'That showed true courage.'

'I loved that bit when the hero nearly got eaten by the space beast,' said Beth, giving Kip a knowing look. 'And then his brilliant assistant talked him through it.'

'And the bit where Zeke Stardancer fell in love with the beautiful Earth woman,' added Stephanie. 'But then duty made him give her up and go off with the much less attractive princess.'

They all looked expectantly at Rose.

'I liked the Special Guest Star best,' she said.

'Sally Lovely turned up?' cried Dad in disbelief.

'Oh, no,' said Kip cheekily. 'We got somebody much better, didn't we?' He looked round at the others and grinned.

'Then . . . who?' asked Dad.

'You'll have to read next week's *Evening Post* to find out,' said Stephanie mysteriously.

Dad scratched his head and stared round at them, noting the secretive smiles on all their faces. 'Did you ever have the feeling you've missed something really important?' he asked – and he must have wondered why they all started laughing.

IN THE SAME SERIES:

NIGHT ON TERROR ISLAND

Have you ever wanted to be in the movies? Kip has, and when he meets mysterious Mr Lazarus he thinks his dream's come true because Mr Lazarus can project people into movies. Films like *Terror Island*, full of hungry sabre-toothed tigers and killer Neanderthals.

Can Kip rescue his sister before the sabre-toothed tigers get her? And if he can – how is he going to get back?!

9781849392709 £5.99

SPY ANOTHER DAY

After the thrills and spills of his adventure on Terror Island, Kip is reluctant to allow Mr Lazarus to send him into another movie. But Beth has other ideas when she discovers The Paramount is planning to show the latest film in the Jason Corder series, *Spy Another Day*.

Can they find their way through all the dangers of a spy movie and defeat the evil genius, Doctor Leo Kasabian, before the final credits roll and they are trapped there ... forever?

'The thrills just keep on coming ... it's a cracker!' *Bookbag*

9781849394178 £5.99